I0691412

WHO IS THE DADDY?

First Edition

Published by The Nazca Plains Corporation
Las Vegas, Nevada
2014

ISBN: 978-1-61098-377-8

Ebook ISBN: 978-1-61098-378-5

Published by

The Nazca Plains Corporation ®

4640 Paradise Rd, Suite 141

Las Vegas NV 89109-8000

PUBLISHER'S NOTE

Who is the Daddy? is a work of fiction created wholly by *Lew Bull*'s imagination. All characters are fictional and any resemblance to any persons living or deceased is purely by accident. No portion of this book reflects any real person or events.

Cover, CURAphotography

Art Director, Blake Stephens

To all those who enjoy a Daddy/son
relationship - care for each other!

WHO IS THE DADDY?

First Edition

Lew Bull

CONTENTS

CHAPTER 1

Let me introduce myself. My name is Nathan and I live in the heart of Fort Lauderdale, Florida. I was born a nice Jewish boy who grew up in a nice Jewish family that adhered to nice Jewish rules and norms and had nice Jewish relatives. Now, although I am an adult and still Jewish, I am not so nice when it comes to dealing with the relatives or adhering to the Jewish rules and norms, but I am nice to the young boys I meet.

Like any nice Jewish boy growing up, my relatives had an influence on my later life and although I had a number of aunts and uncles, there was one who stood out among them. Uncle Cecil always gave me sweets, ice creams, clothes, money and blowjobs. It was he who taught me to suck the sherbet out of a sherbet stick, as he called it, and to enjoy it; naturally, some 'sticks' were bigger than others and some longer than others, but I always found I managed to get the 'sherbet' out.

Uncle Cecil was not married and when I was eighteen, and he was in his late thirties, he took me on a holiday to Chicago. He said it was a business trip but I soon found out what Uncle Cecil meant by 'business'. Most of our days were spent shopping, as he had a passion for fashion and that was how my wardrobe managed to grow, but in the evenings, that's when the 'business' transactions took place.

One evening, he took me off to a bar and I was introduced to his methods of conducting business. Uncle Cecil, who was relatively good looking and had a bubbly personality, seemed to surround himself with young men and what intrigued me was that these young men actually flocked to him like ducks take to water. It was as if he had a magnetic appeal. I could not understand what it was that was attracting these young men to him, so I asked; after all, I needed to learn if I was to survive in the world of Uncle Cecil.

"Dress well, have money, keep in good shape and know what to do with your dick," said Uncle Cecil sagely.

I could understand what he meant by the clothes, keeping in good shape, having money, but I was not sure what he meant by knowing what to do with my dick.

"My boykie, you have been blessed by being Jewish," he replied, "in other words, you've got so much going for you and you also have something great that you have been given…" He hesitated.

I looked at him in anticipation, waiting to hear what this great thing was and why I was so blessed to be Jewish. He looked at me and realized he would have to spell things out for me.

"Nathan, you have a wonderful big dick – I should know as I taught you how to get sherbet out of a stick – and that is what young men like these, crave for. The other aspects I have mentioned, such as money and the like, are equally important, but when it comes to 'business', it's the size of your dick that counts."

Uncle Cecil stood smiling broadly at me as I stood there taking in what he had said.

He then continued.

"You see, Nathan, these are my boys and to them I'm their Daddy; and what Daddy wants, Daddy gets. They will do anything for me because I've got what they want – a big dick and money."

"And if I didn't have money or a big dick, would that mean I wouldn't be a Daddy when I got older?" I asked naively.

"Of course not," answered Uncle Cecil. "Quite a few of these older guys here probably have small dicks and money or big dicks and no money, but they'll have something that attracts the younger guys, for them to control their boys."

"But I still don't understand the significance of being Jewish," I asked, looking perplexed.

"Dear boy, I know a lot of men are circumcised who are not Jewish, but you see not only do you have a perfect specimen of a dick, but it's that you also have the refined Jewish good looks and money."

That was my basic introduction to the world of Uncle Cecil, and now at the ripe age of forty, I have done exactly what Uncle Cecil had instructed. From our first trip together to Chicago when I was eighteen, I have been going to gym to build up my body, kept myself fit and build up my bank balance. As for my dick, well that grew but it did have plenty of exercise to strengthen that muscle. My hair had taken on a few gray streaks, especially in the temple area, but apart from that, it remained a light brown-blond color. I had also maintained my tan without letting the sun's rays age my skin too much. To sum up, I think I looked eligible and attractive, and Uncle Cecil seemed happy by what he saw as he still managed to get the sherbet out of my stick and I out of his stick.

I am following Uncle Cecil's example and on occasions, he is following my example as we share the odd times together. I have now become a Daddy and these are some of my adventures.

CHAPTER 2

On my twentieth birthday, Uncle Cecil arranged a party for me in his Fort Lauderdale apartment and invited a number of his young men, or boys, as he liked to call them, even though they were not really in their teens.

"You're no longer a teenager," he said, "so you're eligible to mix with the men now."

I was flattered to be in the same category as him and was pleasantly surprised to see the array of young men that he had attracted over the years. Naturally, there were some of his older friends along with their boys, so it tended to be an evening of Daddies and their boys. Of course, I had no Daddy of my own so Uncle Cecil took me under his wing for the evening, not that I really wanted to have a Daddy as such. I was of the opinion that I was the dominant person in a relationship, except of course with Uncle Cecil, although there were times when I was with him.

At the party, I watched how the older men behaved with their boys and how they treated them. A couple had arrived dressed in leather; the Daddies in leather jeans, waistcoats or harnesses with their boys in similar dress and wearing dog collars attached to chains. Although I did not like the idea of being dragged around by someone, their appearances in leather were certainly a turn on for me. The sight, touch and smell of the leather made me aroused and I told Uncle Cecil at one stage during the evening of my feelings. One Daddy had on a pair of leather chaps over his leather jockstrap, a leather harness over his buffed chest and leather straps tightly bound around each bicep. In his hand, he had a leash attached to a studded collar around the neck of a young boy who looked about nineteen, but Uncle Cecil said he was twenty-two.

"That looks hot," I whispered to Uncle Cecil when we were alone in the kitchen of his apartment where the party was being held.

"Do you mean the Daddy or the boy?" asked Uncle Cecil.

"The Daddy," I whispered back, as some of the guests entered the kitchen.

"That's Frank," replied Uncle Cecil. "He's fifty-five and they've been together for about six months, but they're very into S & M, if that turns you on."

"I just thought that the way he was dressed and with his well-kept body, he looked very sexy," I quipped. "But he certainly doesn't look fifty-five."

"You see what I told you about looking after yourself, and then the boys will flock to you – just the same way that you're showing an interest."

Frank looked very manly both in his attire and his physical manner and this fascinated me. I had no objections to guys who were a little effeminate, but I found the guys who were manly more attractive to me.

"Frank!" shouted Uncle Cecil, "Have you actually met my nephew Nathan?"

Frank headed towards us dragging his boy behind him.

"No, Cecil, but I can see where he gets his good looks from. Hi I'm Frank," he said extending his hand to me.

I took his hand to shake and felt the firm grip he had. As he squeezed my hand, I could see his bicep tense and form a very pleasing muscle to see. His smile was genuine and he held my hand for an unusually long time, squeezing all the time.

"And what do you do, Nathan?" asked Frank while still holding my hand.

"I'm in advertising," I volunteered.

"Good place to be. All the beautiful people seem to get drawn into that field. Do you remember that pretty boy Josh?" enquired Frank, letting go of my hand and turning to Uncle Cecil.

Uncle Cecil looked somewhat bewildered at first.

"You know the one who stayed with me for about two months and then went off to New York."

"Oh yes!" said Uncle Cecil once Frank had given him more information on Josh.

"Great ass," continued Frank, "and loved to be fucked. The way that he would grind that cute ass of his on my dick would send me to heaven every time. That boy knew how to use his talents." He laughed and then continued. "There were times when he couldn't get enough of my dick and I would have to push him away so I could recover."

He then turned to me as he said this.

"Don't think I can't take the pace, Nathan, but a guy's dick has to recover occasionally, it's just that Josh never gave me time before he was raring to go again. I think he would qualify as a sex-starved young man."

All of us laughed.

"Do you ever see him, Frank?" asked Uncle Cecil.

"Oh yes, about three or four times a year."

"Does he come to visit you here?" continued Uncle Cecil.

"Yes! Why, do you want him the next time he comes to visit?"

"Well, I wouldn't mind," replied Uncle Cecil, with a glint in his eye. "That is, if you're not going to be using that hot ass of his."

Frank laughed heartily.

"I've got a new ass to fuck, as you see," he said, dragging his boy on the chain, a little closer to us.

I smiled at the young man who simply glared back at me. I was not sure whether he thought I was after his Daddy or not, but the look was not of a happy person. I decided to leave Frank and Uncle Cecil, along with the young man, to carry on discussing the assets of Josh and head back into the lounge where the other guests were now dancing and chatting.

A gray-haired, stocky man of about sixty approached me and asked if I was the birthday boy.

"Yes," I replied and smiled.

"Do I get to kiss the birthday boy then?" he enquired.

Before I had a chance to respond, his lips were firmly planted on mine and I felt his tongue fighting to enter my mouth. I kept my lips firmly clamped close and then I felt his hands groping my ass and his fat stomach grinding against mine, obviously trying to rub his dick against mine. The only difference was that I could not even feel a dick there. I think his stomach protruded so far that it overhung his dick. I broke free and gasped for air.

"You've got a fine body, birthday boy, and a fine ass. I'd love to fuck that ass of yours."

I was taken aback by his straightforwardness and without being rude, excused myself on the pretext that I had to get something from the kitchen, and headed hastily back to Frank and Uncle Cecil.

"We wondered where you'd gone to," said Uncle Cecil, seeing my panic-stricken face. "Are you all right?"

"Yes," I gasped, then whispering so hopefully Frank did not overhear me, said, "just about raped by some fat old guy."

Uncle Cecil roared with laughter when he heard what had happened.

"Oh Nathan, don't take too much notice of Gerry, he's just a desperate old man, but quite harmless."

"Harmless!" I exclaimed. "He was about to rape me, I think."

Both Frank and Uncle Cecil now laughed together.

"Nathan, he wouldn't know where his dick is," said Frank. "That stomach of his always gets in the way so the boys know that their asses are safe."

As Frank said this, he gave the huge bulge in his jockstrap a squeeze and I could see that he had a pair of hefty balls and probably an equally hefty dick. He saw me looking and smiled.

"Now this is what you call a dick," he proudly said, hoisting his package up by placing his hand under the bulge and pushing up.

"He's not joking," Confirmed Uncle Cecil, "and I should know."

They laughed together again like two old men reminiscing. The chained boy continued to look sullen and unhappy and I felt as if I wanted to cut the chain and let him go free to enjoy himself.

Eventually, the chained boy spoke up. I think this might have been the first time he had spoken all night.

"Please can we dance?" he asked.

"Oh yes, of course," said Frank, as if he had only suddenly been reminded that he had someone attached to him.

Frank and his boy went back into the lounge while I remained with Uncle Cecil.

"He fancies you, Nathan," said Uncle Cecil.

"Who?"

"Frank. He asked if you were my boy and I told him you were not anyone's. Then he said he wouldn't mind getting that ass of yours."

I laughed.

"My ass isn't available for anyone."

"Oh! Not even me?"

"You're family and I owe you big time for what I've learnt, so that's different. In any case, he has his boy. What's wrong with him?"

"I think you can see the boy's not really interested in being here so he was considering in sending him out on his own for the night and staying to enjoy the evening alone."

I did not know what to say. Sure, I honestly did think that Frank looked incredibly sexy in what he was wearing and his body was taut and well defined for someone his age, but was I willing to have him ravage my ass!

The evening progressed and later people started to drift off, probably to other parties, but Frank remained without his boy. By midnight, there was only Frank, Uncle Cecil, fat Gerry and myself left at the party.

"Gerry, are you going home alone?" questioned Frank.

"Probably," replied the overweight man.

"Why don't you take a trip to one of the clubs," continued Frank, "you're bound to pick someone up there."

Gerry's face lit up at the thought, hastily excused himself and set off in search of any of the clubs where he might have some success.

"Nathan, won't you make some coffee for us, please?" requested Uncle Cecil.

I made my way into the kitchen and started to make the coffee. The percolator had not boiled yet when Frank came into the kitchen alone.

"Do you need a hand, Nathan?"

"Oh, no thanks Frank. Everything's under control," I replied. "You go and relax with Uncle Cecil."

"I'd rather be here with you," said Frank coming up behind me, putting his muscular arms around my waist, and pressing his firm, hefty bulge up against my ass.

I did not know what to do as I did find the man attractive, but I was not sure whether I wanted to be fucked by the guy in the same way he might do it to his boy. Even though he was half-naked, he exuded intense warmth that I could feel through my clothing. I could feel my dick begin to stir in my briefs, but tried to push my lustful thoughts from my mind. Before I had much of a chance to decide what to do, Frank had spun me around to face him and I felt his erection pressed up hard against mine.

"Hmm! That feels good," he said as his mouth moved closer to mine and then I felt his lips touch mine.

As if by magic, my mouth automatically opened to welcome his tongue into my mouth. He pressed his mouth harder against mine and soon I had my arms around his waist while his hands ripped open the zip to my jeans, shucked them and my briefs to the floor and hoisted me onto the kitchen counter. He hoisted my legs, pulling off my sneakers and then my jeans and briefs. With my legs still in the air, his mouth found my hard dick and smothered it with long, deep sucking. His tongue, after a while, ventured towards my balls taking each one into his mouth and rolling them around with his tongue, and then he set off in search of my puckering hole. He found it quickly and rimmed me causing me to groan loudly. All the while, his free hand stroked my dick, allowing his spit from his sucking to lubricate my mushroom-shaped cock head. The sensation was erotically orgasmic. I felt his thick thumb enter my ass and begin to massage the interior, then another finger joined in and soon he had three fingers spreading my opening. I'm glad that he did that because when he pulled down his jockstrap to release his balls and dick, I could see what was about to enter my pulsating ass. Frank was also cut and had a long, thick cock with a large head. I felt it push up against my opening and instinctively I closed down, but his determination was great. He pushed harder and I tried to resist his size, but eventually gave in. As his huge cock head made its way past my sphincter, I cried out but he never stopped. He sank his full length slowly into my waiting chute. I could see stars in front of me as I felt my chute being stretched wider to accommodate his size. Frank was big! Once he had sunk right in up to the hilt, I felt his pendulous balls slap against my ass, then he began a slow but rhythmic in and out thrust. Slowly I began to become accustomed to his size and with that, began to enjoy the pleasure that was overcoming my whole being. He increased his pace and with each thrust there was an audible grunt from Frank as he pushed deeply into me and with it, a gasp emitted from me. As he held my legs aloft, I took hold of my engorged, leaking dick and, using my pre-cum, slicked up my dick while I stroked myself. Our groans and moans increased in volume, both of us oblivious of Uncle Cecil sitting in the lounge waiting for his coffee, and soon Frank's pace increased with ferocity and I knew he was nearing his climax, but so was I.

A loud, prolonged groan came from Frank's throat and he fired into my ass. His thrusts became frenetic and I could see he had both eyes shut with a satisfied smile on his face. I gripped my cock and squeezed as I felt the first stream of cum rising from my balls. A spray shot out of the tip of my cock and landed on my chest, quickly followed by another and another until there was just a trickle of warm cum oozing from the tip and running onto my stomach.

As our breathing reverted to a form of normality, Frank opened his eyes and his smile broadened.

"You sure would make someone a good boy, Nathan. Happy birthday, kid."

He leant across my body, his cock still firmly embedded in my ass, and kissed me gently on the lips, and then he slowly began to pull out of my ass. With a 'plop', his semi-hard cock emerged and my hole slammed shut and I was able to lower my legs. Frank helped me to my feet where I was able to pull on my briefs, jeans and sneakers while he pulled his jockstrap over his still large cock.

"I wonder if Uncle Cecil's gone to bed, or if he's still waiting for his coffee."

Both Frank and I chuckled and began to pour our coffee.

As we entered the lounge, Uncle Cecil gave both of us a knowing smile.

"Is the coffee still hot?" he enquired. "I thought I might have to come and make it myself."

"We were busy making it," I replied.

Uncle Cecil merely smiled back.

"I know you were making it, as you call it, but did you enjoy it?"

I blushed but Frank merely sat himself down next to Uncle Cecil on the sofa.

"He's a good fuck, Cecil. You've trained him well."

I smiled at the compliment.

"Thanks Frank, but he's still got a lot to learn if he's going to be someone's boy one day," said Uncle Cecil, admiringly.

"Well, I can tell you that I wouldn't mind having him as my boy, that is if he'd be willing to be it," replied Frank, winking at me.

I was not sure what entailed being someone's boy.

"If it means being dragged around by the neck, no thanks," I blurted. "I'm not having some dog collar or chain wrapped around my neck."

Both Frank and Uncle Cecil roared with laughter.

"No Nathan, not all boys do that," said Frank, reassuringly. "Sam, the young boy that I came to the party with is very into that sort of thing and he likes it if I totally dominate him, but I haven't done that to all my boys."

"You mean you've got others?" I enquired.

"Let's just say that I have some for different occasions. Sam, for example is into rough stuff and serious S&M, which I offer him, but then I've got a couple of others who prefer gentle, safe stuff."

"What constitutes 'safe' stuff, as you put it?" I asked.

"Well if they're disobedient, I put them over my knee and give them a hiding."

"You mean like you would do to a child?"

"Exactly," interrupted Uncle Cecil.

"Pull their shorts down and whack their plum asses because they've been naughty boys; and they love it," continued Frank. "Would you like me to show you?"

"No thanks!" I exclaimed. "I value my ass," pretending to make a mock escape. "But I've always thought that Daddies were very old men who couldn't make it with a guy."

"Not at all," replied Uncle Cecil, indignantly. "You get young men who have a passion for even younger guys and want to treat them like they are their own sons, then on the other hand you get young guys who possibly have had a bad childhood with their fathers, who look up to older guys as role model fathers, if you get what I mean."

"If you take Sam," said Frank, "he comes from a split family and was brought up by his mother; so he had no father-figure in the home and when we first met, he saw me in the role of a father and that's why he likes to be treated like my son."

"What attracted you to Frank, Nathan?" asked Uncle Cecil, getting up to pour himself another cup of coffee.

I thought for a moment and then said, "I think it was his appearance."

"What do you mean by that – his clothes or his physical appearance?"

"I think it was both," I answered. "I liked his rugged manly look, but that was also enhanced by his leather."

"If you took the leather away from me," questioned Frank, "would you still have been attracted to me?"

"Yes!" I replied confidently.

"But why?" continued Uncle Cecil.

"I think it was just his more mature look and I thought, how well kept he looked for someone his age."

"Thanks very much!" retorted Frank, "someone his age. How old do you think I look? Seventy-five?"

"No, no. I didn't mean it like that," I professed, apologetically. "What I meant was that for someone who was middle-aged you had kept your body in good shape."

"But you were quite happy for a middle-aged man to fuck you?" asked Frank.

"In your case, yes," I replied.

"Why?" continued Uncle Cecil, still trying to get the real reason out of me. "Did you see Frank as a father substitute?"

I contemplated this idea for a while, and then nodded.

"I suppose you're right, Uncle Cecil. It's not that I never had a father in my life, but I did feel warmth from Frank when we were together that I've never experienced from my own father."

"You must understand that's quite different. I'm sure that your father had not intention or desire to fuck you," said Frank, chuckling as he said it, "but I did and it was more than just that. I felt that I wanted to embrace you in my arms as protect you in a way."

I remained quiet as he explained his feelings. I felt honored and touched by what he had said and was glad that Uncle Cecil had invited Frank to my birthday party. I sat looking at both men and wondered if at some stage in their lives they had ever had a Daddy/

son relationship. I decided to put that thought into my memory for a later time but I was definitely going to ask.

"Well," said Frank rising from the sofa in which he had been sitting. "I suppose I'd better make my way home and leave you two lovely men to clean up and head to bed."

We said our goodbyes, and Frank gave me an extra special hug that almost squeezed the life out of me before he set off home. Uncle Cecil and I quickly cleaned up the apartment and made our way to our bedrooms, but before I went to bed, I had to get clarity in my mind.

"Uncle Cecil, were you and Frank ever in a Daddy-son relationship?"

He smiled as though deep in thought, then he turned to me, kissed me on the cheek and said, "Now get to bed my boy."

CHAPTER 3

I awoke early and got out of bed, padded my way through to Uncle Cecil's kitchen to make some coffee and then, once it was made, I went quietly into his room to see if he was awake. He was lying in bed with his eyes open smiling at me.

"Hop in, kid."

I put the coffee cups down on each side table and hopped in next to Uncle Cecil. His body was naked yet warm and I snuggled up closer to him, feeling his arms around me in a caring, loving manner. He pulled me closer to him and I felt safe and comfortable.

"So how was last night?" he asked; a broad smile on his face.

"It was great, thanks. In addition, thank you so much, for the wonderful party you gave me. There were quite a few interesting looking people there."

"All my friends are interesting," replied Uncle Cecil. "And Frank?"

I remained silent, thinking about Frank and the previous night.

"He likes you, you know," continued Uncle Cecil.

"Hm, I get the feeling you're right."

"I think he'd love to have you as his boy," said Uncle Cecil, squeezing me even closer to him.

"Maybe," I absent-mindedly said, "but tell me more about him."

"Oh dear, where do I start!"

Uncle Cecil then went into a long discourse on Frank and how Frank had come into his life and what had happened between the two of them.

They had first met when Uncle Cecil was twenty and Frank was thirty-five. Uncle Cecil had been in a bar and Frank had approached him and picked him up for the night. Frank was taken by the young man's beauty, just as much as Uncle Cecil was taken in by Frank's physical manliness and sex appeal.

"He had the sexiest little moustache when I first met him," said Uncle Cecil, his eyes going into a dream-like state, "and his body was more defined, not that he's lost any of that definition. His hair had no gray in it and was slicked back, ever so smart. He just looked rugged and you wanted to be ravaged by the man."

I chuckled as he said the 'ravaged' part, as that is exactly how I felt when Frank had me over the kitchen table.

"Oh, he was a good lover," continued Uncle Cecil, "and still is. He cared for me and acted like my protector. If anyone said anything derogatory to me, Frank was there to defend me. He just had to puff out his chest and they'd run a mile," said Uncle Cecil, chuckling to himself.

"You're very fond of Frank, aren't you?"

He turned and smiled at me.

"Oh yes. I'd say he's probably my best friend."

"So were you two in a steady relationship?"

"Yes, you could say that. He was my Daddy and he treated me well. Sure I got the occasional spanking for being a naughty boy, but he never treated me badly."

"Then what happened? I mean you're not with him anymore, so what happened?"

"Well, you can see we're still close but he found someone younger and I realized that I was becoming more interested in a younger man, so I was becoming like a Daddy to others, like you, for instance."

At that, he turned to me and kissed my forehead. Instantaneously I snuggled like a child into his body and felt his erection prod my stomach. We lay together not speaking and I could feel the gentle throbs of his dick, which was now making me hard. I decided to wriggle down under the bedclothes and head towards his waiting cock. My mouth opened and surrounded the mushroom-shaped head as I took his cock deep into my throat. I could hear Uncle Cecil moaning gently as I worked my mouth over his length until eventually I heard him gasp and felt the warm liquid enter my mouth. I swallowed rapidly as the next load came firing out. I continued providing pleasure for him until I had sucked him dry, then I surfaced from under the bedclothes to see him smiling broadly at me and cuddling me once more in his arms.

"You're such a good boy, Nathan; you'd make any Daddy happy."

I felt proud and pleased that I had brought some happiness to Uncle Cecil who was like my Daddy.

"But tell me more about Frank."

"Well, he's got a younger brother but apparently they came from a family that traveled a great deal. I think he once said his father was businessman and the work took him all over the country. This meant that apart from all the moving, they did not see their father that often. It also meant that when they were growing up, his parents were more preoccupied with their careers than with their family, so the boys were left to their own devices most of the time. I know that Frank said he was once arrested for causing a disturbance in the neighborhood when he was about seventeen or eighteen, but his family did not seem bothered by that. I also know that he tended to look after his younger brother."

"You mean like he took over the father role with his brother?"

"Yes. I think that is when Frank realized how he enjoyed that role. I am not saying that he and his brother became lovers or anything like that. I just think that they shared their brotherly love in a slightly different way that other brothers might do. He did tell me once that they had often spent evenings together and he would hold his brother lovingly in his arms as though to protect him and that this would leads to them having sex together."

"So his brother's also gay?" I questioned.

"Oh yes, but he lives in New York. I know that he often comes here for holidays and when they get together, it's almost like when he and I get together."

"And what does that entail?" I asked.

"You mean Frank and me?"

"Yes"

"Well, you know! I become his boy for the night."

I smiled at the thought of Uncle Cecil being Frank's boy, but I could understand why he might enjoy being with Frank. Frank just had that all-encompassing sex appeal, that rugged manliness and the desire to want to be taken by him.

"Why didn't Frank stay last night, then?"

"I'm not sure, but my gut feeling was that he didn't want to upset either of us."

"Meaning?"

"Well, you know now that I was once a boy of his and he's very interested in you becoming his boy, so perhaps he didn't want to upset either of us," said Uncle Cecil, sagely.

"We could have shared him," I answered flippantly.

Uncle Cecil laughed heartily.

"I quite agree with you and that would have been fun, but I don't suppose he thought of that."

Just then, the telephone in Uncle Cecil's apartment rang.

"Shall I get it?" I volunteered.

"No, don't you worry, I'll get it, after all I must get up." Uncle Cecil slid from the bed and headed towards the ringing telephone. He picked up the receiver.

"Cecil Stein speaking… of hi Frank… how are you … hung over or not? No we're both awake – Nathan made coffee and brought it to me in bed… no nothing happened, we just had coffee and spoke about you in fact… oh nothing too exciting… just about you… what a great guy you are…no, I'm serious, he does think you're great…"

I entered the lounge where Uncle Cecil was still talking to Frank on the phone.

"In fact he's just walked into the lounge now… would you like to speak to him?"

"Frank wants to speak to you," he said, handing me the receiver.

"Hi Frank, how are you? … I'm fine thanks, and thanks again for last night, I appreciate you coming to my birthday… we've got nothing planned for today, or should I say I don't have anything planned, but I'm not sure about Uncle Cecil…"

"…I'm free," retorted Uncle Cecil.

"He says he's free… at the moment? Well he's naked and I'm wearing my jocks…"

"What's Frank want to know that for?" queried Uncle Cecil.

I placed my hand over the mouthpiece and replied to Uncle Cecil, "he asked what we were wearing."

"Oh."

"I think if you give us about an hour, we should be ready… that sounds like fun… sure, I'll tell him…thanks Frank… see you soon… cheers."

I replaced the telephone receiver.

"What's Frank up to now?" enquired Uncle Cecil.

"He's coming by in an hour to pick us up and we're going out with him."

"Where to?"

"He just said to dress casually and bring a bathing suit and towel."

"Sounds like we're off to the beach," said Uncle Cecil, casually.

"I don't think so," I replied.

"So you do know where we're going, then?"

I nodded and smiled back.

"So, spill the beans."

"We're going sailing."

"Sailing!" exclaimed Uncle Cecil. "In what? The Queen Mary 2?"

"Nothing as grand as that. I think he's organized a yacht or something."

"But, he knows I get seasick."

"Come on Uncle Cecil, you won't get seasick, it's such a calm day and in any case I'm sure that Frank has considered that, if he's aware of it and won't do anything to harm you."

"I suppose you're right, my boy. Did he say if any others were going to be there?"

"No. never mentioned a word. He just said he'd pick us up and head to the marina."

We headed back to our rooms to get ready and after slipping on a Speedo, which Uncle Cecil lent me, which was a little small for what I had to pack into it, and pulling on a vest and pair of shorts, I was ready.

"Are you ready?" I shouted to the other bedroom.

"Of course not. It takes me time to get ready."

I wandered into Uncle Cecil's room and there he was with five shirts laid out on his bed.

"I just can't think of which one to wear."

I laughed and added," You are worse than an old woman. Just take any one of them as you're only going to wear it to the boat because once we're on board, I'm sure that you'll whip it off."

"Yes but it must be coordinated with my longs."

"And what color are those?"

"White."

I became exasperated.

"Uncle Cecil, white goes with everything, so it doesn't matter what color shirt you pull on, but hurry up, Frank will be here soon."

He glanced at me, shook his head and grabbed a shirt, which he hurriedly put on. Before the hour was up, Frank was ringing the front door bell. He looked very sporty with a white vest over his tanned, buffed chest and a pair of white shorts tightly encasing a well-formed package that left nothing to the imagination. He looked sexy as usual.

"Are you guys ready," said a chirpy Frank, giving me a wink.

"Old mother hen is ready now, but we had a battle to get the old thing clothes to wear," I sarcastically said.

"I know exactly what you mean, Nathan. I've been through all that with Cecil and nothing changes."

The three of us headed off to the marina, with Uncle Cecil constantly asking where we were going, and Frank replying that he must wait and see.

We arrived at the marina, parked the car and headed in the direction that Frank was going. We arrived at a very elegant and quite large, white yacht. On the deck, waiting for us was a young man in his late twenties, dressed all in white. He welcomed us aboard and Frank soon introduced us to him. His name was Marc and it was apparently his family's yacht, so he would be taking us out for our cruise.

Marc seemed an amiable young man and once we had climbed on board, we set sail, so to speak, although this yacht had no sails; it was a motorized yacht with cabins and a lounge and a galley.

Up on deck were an array of snacks and drinks and soon Marc, was encouraging us to tuck into the food and drinks.

"Who's this guy?" I asked Uncle Cecil when we were alone.

"I have no idea, but I do like his boat."

Soon, we were speeding out into the ocean and heading down the coast as though we were going to Miami. After a short while, the speed decreased and soon we came to a halt in the middle of the sea.

"And now?" asked Uncle Cecil, who had not mentioned anything about seasickness or shown any signs of being sick.

"We're stopping here," replied Marc, who had switched off the engine, dropped anchor and come to join us with our snacks and drinks.

I must admit, it was very pleasant to sit bobbing on the gentle sea, indulging in fine snacks and good drinks. During the conversations, I managed to pick up that Marc was at university and was spending the weekend at his parent's holiday cottage. Obviously, his parents were well off to own such a yacht and I imagined that their 'beach cottage' was probably a mansion. It also transpired that Frank had only recently met Marc and had become friends. I wondered if Marc was another of his boys but was not about to enquire. Uncle Cecil also seemed to be in the dark so to speak about Marc, but I did notice that he was giving the young man more than a few admiring glances.

After a couple of drinks, Marc pulled his shorts and top off to reveal a Speedo and promptly dived into the blue sea. He was soon followed by Frank who had on a white Speedo that revealed everything he had underneath. Uncle Cecil and I both looked at each other in awe by what we had seen and both smiled to each other, knowingly.

"Come on you two," shouted Frank when he surfaced having dived from the yacht.

Uncle Cecil and I both hastily followed, and the four of us swam around like happy fish. The water was cool and refreshing and the sun's rays beat down on us in the water. After some time of splashing around, we emerged from the sea and found places on the deck to lie down and tan under the sun's gaze. Both Uncle Cecil and I watched as Frank emerged from the sea. His white Speedo clung tightly to his body, outlining the thick dick that lay passively under the Lycra material. I know my mouth watered when I saw that and I was sure that Uncle Cecil's did likewise.

Marc had gone down below the deck when he climbed on board and grabbed a towel which he brought up onto the deck and found a spot to lie on.

"Won't you get me a drink?" asked Frank of Marc.

"I'll get one for you in a moment. I just want to get some sun."

"Daddy would like a drink now please."

"I'll get one in a moment, Daddy. I told you."

"Listen! Who's your daddy?"

"You are," replied Marc, a little indignantly.

"So get one for your daddy or you'll feel my hand."

During this conversation, both Uncle Cecil and I kept quiet but eyed each other. The thought that crossed my mind was how many boys did Frank have and if he wanted me to be one of them, where did I fit in?

Marc gave a deep sigh, hauled his young body into a standing position, and went to make Frank a martini. He returned with the drink, placed it on the deck where Frank was lying and returned to his towel. The look on Frank's face was that of an angry man, but he never said anything. Silence reigned over the yacht while the swells in the sea continued to make a gentle rise and fall movement with the boat.

When Frank had finished drinking his martini, he rose and called Marc to, "come below, I want to speak to you."

Marc reluctantly rose and followed. Again, Uncle Cecil and I merely looked at one another.

There was a moment of silence and then we both heard the "thwack" sound of something hitting something else. This was quickly followed by a few more 'hitting' sounds and the voice of Marc, cry out after each "thwack". A smile appeared on Uncle Cecil's face as he realized what might be happening. I also began to realize and found it strange that after each "thwack" I found myself becoming aroused, knowing what the two men were probably doing. I also became envious of Marc and wished it was my ass that was being punished and my ass that might get the pleasure of feeling that huge dick eventually slide into it. The sounds of smacking stopped and then we heard the low moans and groans emanating from one of the cabins below. This continued for some time and throughout that my dick got harder and harder until I could not control myself anymore and rolled onto my back allowing Uncle Cecil to see the state I was in.

"I know the feeling my boy," he replied, sliding his hand over his equally engorged cock.

"I think I'm going for another swim to try to cool down," I said, diving overboard and splashing into the cool sea.

I swam around for a while and as I climbed the steps leading back onto the boat, I heard the cries of Marc as he shouted, "Yes, Daddy, oh yes. Fuck me hard, Daddy."

Then both men cried out as they obviously came together, and then there was silence. It was some time later that they both emerged from below and dived straight into the sea. Uncle Cecil and I once more smiled to each another and never said a word about what we had heard.

My mind was now confused because I did not understand fully how the Daddy/son scenarios worked. Could a Daddy have many sons or boys and if so how did he have relationships with them or were they merely his fuck buddies. If this was the case, I wasn't entirely happy about just being someone's fuck buddy.

We continued our floating aimlessly in the sea, swimming and drinking until the sun began to set and then we headed back to the marina. We thanked Marc for allowing us on his yacht and Frank drove us back to Uncle Cecil's apartment. He didn't come up with us and when Uncle Cecil and I had settled in for a well-deserved cup of coffee each, we sat down to discuss the day's events.

"Well, Nathan, what did you think of today?"

I didn't want to say anything that might upset Uncle Cecil regarding Frank's behavior, although whom he chooses to fuck is his business and not mine, but I did say that I wasn't sure about the idea of me becoming Frank's boy.

"Why not, Nathan?"

"I don't know Uncle Cecil; it's just that I don't really know the guy. I mean, what does he do for a living, for example?"

"He's a television producer."

I was stunned.

"A TV producer?"

"Yes, a TV producer," reiterated Uncle Cecil, "and a very handsome one at that."

I must confess that I did have a passion, not known by many, for men in the entertainment trade; just as some have passions for guys in uniforms. Therefore, the idea of Frank being a TV producer did stir a little in my mind; but on the other hand, did I want to be the next 'victim' on the casting couch?

CHAPTER 4

At the advertising agency, where I worked, my boss had called me into his office and asked me if I was willing to go to Paris, France to work on an advertising campaign. To be asked if I wanted to travel was a bonus for my job as I spent most of my time cocooned in an office doing the occasional graphic designs and some copy writing for various products being advertised.

"Are you serious?" I asked disbelievingly.

"Of course, if you don't want to do it, I'll offer it to someone else in the office."

"No, no, no!" I exclaimed. "I'll gladly do it, but when were you thinking of sending me?"

"Next week. You will meet up with a company and work with them. The reason they need someone from here is that the advert calls for an English-speaking person to write the English copy for the advert and to help in the design of the English version of the advert.

It is going to be a television and print advert, so you will probably be there for about a week. Do you think you can do it?"

"Sure, but don't they have anyone to do the English for them?"

"They asked for an English speaker as most of them battle with the language. Obviously, the French version of the advert will be no problem for them. All you'll have to do is write the English copy and advise on any nuances that might crop up in the process."

I became very excited as I had never been to France before and although Uncle Cecil had, he had always spoken of Paris's beauty and how the men were sexy. He did, however, once mention to me that on a visit to Paris, he had had enormous trouble trying to communicate, as he did not speak French. This stuck in the back of my mind and I began to worry that I would also have the same problem.

"What about communication?" I asked my boss.

"We've organized for you to meet with one of their staff – a Mr. Toulon, who can speak some English."

That made me feel a little more comfortable knowing that someone would understand me. As soon as I returned to my office, I phoned Uncle Cecil to tell him. He was as excited as I was and proceeded to tell me what to do and what to watch out for. The questions were flowing from him.

"When are you leaving? Where are you staying? How long are you going for? Do you want addresses? Watch out for the gypsies! If you meet someone you like you won't have to speak French – body language goes a long way."

All I could do was laugh at each question and statement, but throughout, I realized how excited Uncle Cecil was about my impending journey.

"Wait till I tell Frank," he said, slamming down the phone in my ear.

It was not long afterwards that a call came through from Frank, telling me how excited he was as well. He also gave me warnings and advice and said that he knew a couple of French guys but didn't know their addresses. I was not unduly worried that I had no contacts other than the guy from the French advertising agency, and decided that I would make my own arrangements with regard to my evening entertainment when I got there. Prior to leaving Florida, I bought a travel book on Paris so I could see what there was to see there. From the pictures in the book, I was becoming more and more excited to be going.

The day of my flight arrived and like a child on a first journey, I was so excited. Uncle Cecil took me to the airport and all the way there, he kept up a barrage of questions.

"Have you got condoms? Do you have lube? Do you have your camera? Have you enough money? What about underwear?"

He sounded like my mother, except for the lube and the condoms, but I appreciated his concerns for me. Naturally my answers to all his questions was 'yes' but it still didn't satisfy him as he continued with things like, 'be careful where you go at night', 'don't go down any dark alleys', and such like.

I boarded the evening flight and soon we were winging our way across the Atlantic towards Europe. I had been booked on an Air France flight so from the time we took off I was immersed in a culture of French food and language, although they did speak English as well. I eyed a couple of the air stewards and wondered if I should ask them about any clubs, bars and the like, but then I felt that maybe on the plane wasn't the place to ask these things. Uncle Cecil had

photocopied a page from a book he had which included the names
and addresses of some bars and clubs in Paris, so I felt a little secure
in the knowledge that I could ask a cab driver to take me there if I so
desired.

As the flight progressed and most of the passengers began
to settle down for the night, I ventured to the rear of the plane and
met with a steward I had eyed earlier. We introduced ourselves and
were soon chatting, in English, to each other. His name was Pierre
and although he wasn't from Paris, he knew it well enough to be
of assistance to me. He wrote down the phone numbers of a couple
of his friends as well as his own. He shared an apartment in Paris
whenever he was stationed there, but his home was in Lyon. He told
me the other person in the apartment was a photographer friend and
that when we landed in Paris he would be staying with his friend for
the next three days before flying off again, and should I like to join
them, they would show me around Paris. I knew that the agency had
arranged accommodation for me but that did not prevent me from
being shown around Paris by a couple of French guys. I did not know
what his friend was like, but I had found Pierre quite attractive, and
he seemed very relaxed to talk to.

Before we landed at Charles de Gaulle Airport in Paris, Pierre
had slipped me a piece of paper with his telephone number on as well
as the address of the apartment he shared, along with the name of his
friend, Marcel.

Once through customs at the airport, I looked out for my contact
to meet me. As I surveyed the faces and placards bearing arriving
passengers' names, I saw a short, balding man, almost disappearing
among the throngs of waiting people, eagerly waving a board with
NATHAN RAUBENHEIMER written on. I headed in his direction

and introduced myself. He had a small, neatly trimmed moustache, slightly stocky body without being portly and a broad smile.

"Welcome to Paris, Mr. Raubenheimer," he said, shaking my hand enthusiastically.

"Hi. Please call me Nathan," I replied feeling the firm grip on my hand.

"Thank you Nathan and I am Claude Toulon, the head of graphic design in our company. Come let us get you to your hotel," he said, leading the way to his vehicle.

On the way to his car, he kept up a constant barrage of questions about my flight, the weather, what Fort Lauderdale was like, the weather, and did I wish to go out at night and what did I expect. I tried as best I could to remain polite but non-descript about what I would really like to do at night.

The drive from the airport to the hotel in the Marais area took quite some time. Admittedly, it was early morning traffic so it was understandable that the journey would take some time. Along the way, Claude kept up his barrage in English, with occasional French outbursts, probably because of either bad driving or slow driving.

We eventually arrived at a small hotel tucked away in a tiny, yet quaint cobble-stoned street. Claude found parking and helped me with my luggage. I booked into the hotel and went upstairs with Claude in tow, to find my room. It was a simply furnished room with a small window overlooking the street below, and had a tiny bathroom attached. Claude seemed happy with the cleanliness of the room and seemed happy that I was happy with the accommodation, so he left for the agency telling me that I would be picked up at 2:00pm that day to meet the others at the agency.

I unpacked and lay down on the soft bed to have a short sleep and recover from the long flight. I did not sleep long and was awakened with the telephone in the room ringing loudly. I answered and it was Claude checking up to see if I had settled in. I was touched by his concern but then I wondered why there was so much attention being given to me. He also said that they were coming to pick me up from the hotel at an earlier time and would I be ready. I assured him that I was ready now so they could come and fetch me.

I went down to the reception area to wait for my transport and soon a young, dark haired man arrived to fetch me. He did not speak much English so our journey tended to be quite silent. On arriving at the agency, I was ushered into a boardroom where I saw Claude. Again, we shook hands and then I was introduced by the other members of the team, who soon arrived in the boardroom. There were five of us who were going to be working on the advert. Claude was leading the group and the young driver who picked me up from the hotel was to be the photographer/cameraman. A vivacious woman of about thirty years of age introduced herself as their copywriter, who I would be working with, and then there was their graphic designer, a young man, by the name of Angelo, who was actually Italian, and finally myself. They all seemed very friendly towards me although they sometimes battled to express themselves in English; however, we made ourselves understood.

We discussed the brief and then set to discussing how we would interpret it. I was quite taken by the enthusiasm of the team, especially Claude. He had created a set of drawings much like a film storyboard, and had obviously discussed all the visual aspects with the young cameraman, whose name was Jacques. After telling Monica, the French copywriter and I what he envisaged, we set to working on the story line for the advert.

I found Monica to be very helpful, explaining what they had in mind, as their immediate audience would be French, and then the international advert would be in English. She drew up a story line, which I found interesting as it dealt with the adventures of a young couple. It was set on a tropical island and they were drinking some wine and feasting on delicious looking food. As the advert was for a brand of wine, the emphasis had to be on the wine and not so much on the food. However, together with the appetizing food and the beautiful setting, it was envisaged that these aspects would attract the viewer to the elegance and beauty of the wine.

We spent the remainder of the afternoon doing our various tasks, and by five that day, Monica and I had created the basis of our copywriting.

"I'll take you back to your hotel, "said Claude, coming to the room in which Monica and I were working.

"Thanks Claude. I appreciate that."

"Are you two nearly finished for the day?" he asked.

We both chorused that we were, and that we were happy with the progress we had made. We closed up our office and Claude drove me back to my hotel. On the way, I politely asked if he would like to join me in a drink, to which he gladly accepted.

The hotel I was staying in had a small intimate bar on the premises so when we arrived back there, Claude and I went into the bar and ordered drinks of beer for me and a brandy for him. As this was my first night in Paris and did not know my way around, I asked Claude if he knew of any restaurants near the hotel. Apparently, there were quite a few so eating was not going to be a problem. Our conversations centered on America, as he had never been there, and he wanted to know more about the nightlife than anything else. This fascinated me, as most people do not focus their enquiries on that if they have never been to a foreign place before. As our conversations continued, I began to wonder if Claude was more of a night person and wondered why he placed so much emphasis on doing things at night, and then it all fell into place.

"My wife isn't interested in going out at night and I enjoy it."

"So what do you do to alleviate the boredom of staying at home every night?" I asked.

Claude blushed somewhat, hesitated then volunteered his answer.

"I go to bars just to mix with other people."

This revelation did not shock me as many people go out alone if their partners are not inclined to do the same things.

"What does your wife say about that?" I asked, wondering if she went out on her own like Claude did.

"She doesn't say anything. We tend to lead separate lives, except if it's a work-related function, then we go out together."

My mind wondered how often Claude did this, but I was not about to enquire.

We drank our drinks and ordered another round. I could see that Claude was becoming more relaxed and comfortable in my company.

"Do you have a wife, back in Florida?" asked Claude.

"No, I'm single," I said, without elaborating.

Claude's face lit up and he seemed more interested in me.

"Do you live with anyone?"

"No, but I spend quite a bit of time with my friends when we get the opportunity," I replied.

He smiled again.

"Do you have many friends?"

"A few but I find I mix more with older guys," I added.

At this, Claude's face beamed.

"Funny, I prefer mixing with younger guys," said Claude easing even more to me.

I wondered if he meant men when he said the word 'guys' but wasn't sure if I should ask him.

"Do you have many older friends, Nathan?"

"Actually I'm very close to an uncle of mine and recently he introduced me to a very nice older man."

The fact that I had said 'older man' made me realize that I had given myself away. Anyone hearing me say those words would have derived a conclusion and come up with the realization that I was gay, and probably into older men.

I noticed that Claude moved his barstool closer to me so that our legs were almost touching. This did not worry me at all, but I did wonder if the other few people in the bar might notice our close proximity. As we finished our second drink, Claude made a suggestion.

"Why don't we go up to your room and have another drink there and then maybe go out for something to eat."

The idea never worried me as I had become quite fond of his company. Claude could not be considered an oil painting, but then he did have a certain *je ne sais quoi*. He was friendly enough, was good looking and I was finding myself getting more and more into liking Daddies. I agreed and we were soon heading up to my room.

On entering the room, I did not even have time to pick up the telephone to order drinks for us, when Claude spun me around and planted his lips on mine, forcing his tongue into my mouth. After the initial shock, I found myself enjoying his passion and was soon fully aroused. I managed to pull away from Claude.

"Sorry, Claude, but I have to go to the bathroom."

He smiled and nodded his head. I went off to the tiny en suite bathroom, and closed the door. After I had finished in there, I reopened the door and went back into the bedroom. Claude was lying naked on top of my bed, smiling at me.

"Come to Daddy," he said as I gazed at his nakedness.

His body was not attractive in the sense that it had definition, but there was something about him that I did not find offensive. His erect cock was of average length and his foreskin had already peeled back to reveal a glistening purplish head. I stood staring and not knowing whether I should join him, but then I thought that if I rejected him outright, he might take offence and I did have to work with him on the project. I decided that I would go along with him as I was feeling aroused.

I slowly peeled off my shirt to reveal my well-formed chest and slim waist. I saw how Claude's face lit up at the sight, and then I unzipped my jeans and pushed them to my ankles. He could see my briefs tenting from my arousal so he knew I was interested. I scuffed off my shoes and slipped out of my jeans. Now I wondered if I should shed the briefs but I thought mystery was a better aphrodisiac, so I kept them on, knowing Claude would be wondering just what was under the thin cotton material. I climbed onto the base of the bed and slowly moved up between his thick legs, aiming for his balls and throbbing cock. As I neared his balls, I lowered my head, stuck out my tongue and proceeded to lick his sweaty balls. After a while, I slid my mouth lower towards his ass hole, but his voice stopped me there.

"Daddy didn't say you could go there!"

I moved back to his balls without saying a word, worked on them some more then headed towards his cock. I licked his full length, licking around the rim of his cock head and hearing him groan, and then I encompassed his cock with my mouth and sank down on it, taking him deep into my throat. His groans became even louder the tighter I sucked on his shaft.

In between the moans and groans, Claude gave an instruction.

"Daddy wants to fuck that beautiful ass of yours."

I was not sure whether I wanted that, so I carried on sucking him.

A more determined and anxious command came from Claude.

"I want that ass. Sit on Daddy's cock!"

I ignored his command and tightened the suction I had created on his cock, causing him to cry out in ecstasy. I suddenly increased my pace and squeezed his balls with my hand. He could not hold on any more. With a loud cry, Claude emptied his juices into my mouth. I sucked and drained his cock, without swallowing his cum. When my mouth was filled with warm cum and I knew he was empty of any more, I released my grip and slowly dribbled his cum over the length of his cock then I began to stroke his cock with his own cum. He was writhing and cooing as I stroked him with his own juices.

"Oh please, stop!" he cried, but I continued.

At length, I slowed down and allowed his whimpering to subside while he continued to enjoy my touch.

"Was that good for you, Daddy?" I asked as I watched his face turn from being ecstatic to one of peace.

He smiled and nodded.

"Maybe next time, you might get my ass, Claude," I said, softly massaging his balls for him.

I went into the bathroom and retrieved a cloth to clean him and then we dressed and headed out for dinner.

"But what about you?" enquired Claude as we headed off. "You didn't come."

"Don't worry about me. It was your pleasure that I was interested in," I replied.

Over dinner, I found Claude becoming extremely friendlier towards me and when we had finished dinner and were heading back to my hotel, I did wonder if he was planning to make a move on me to get to stay the night, or at least part of it.

As we stopped outside the hotel, I thanked Claude for the wonderful evening and told him I was tired after the flight and wanted a relatively early night. He accepted that and we said our 'good nights' and off he went while I made my way up to my room.

CHAPTER 5

The following day at the agency, Monica and I were putting the final changes to our script for the wine advert when Angelo came in and asked if we had heard about Claude.

"No, what's happened?" I asked, worried as I thought he might have had an accident on his way home after leaving my hotel.

"He was arrested last night," reported Angelo.

Both Monica and I were shocked.

"For what?" asked Monica.

"I heard it was drugs," replied Angelo, "but I'm not completely sure."

"Drugs!" I exclaimed. "I wouldn't have thought Claude did drugs."

"As far as I know, he doesn't," said distraught Monica. "Are you sure it was drugs?"

"That's what Jacques told me," answered Angelo.

"How would Jacques know?" continued Monica.

"Apparently he saw Claude last night."

Immediately my mind went into a turmoil as I tried to work out how Jacques could have seen Claude if Claude had been with me. It may have been that Jacques saw him after Claude had left my hotel, but if he had, how would he know what had happened.

"Is Jacques here?" I asked.

"Yes," replied Angelo. "Should I call him in?"

"Yes, please get him," requested Monica.

Angelo disappeared for a moment and soon returned with Jacques who adopted a self-pitying stance.

"Jacques, what happened?" asked an urgent sounding Monica.

"Claude was arrested by the police last night. I think they said it was something about drugs."

"You think… did you hear them say that?" I queried.

"Where was this?" enquired Monica, getting more agitated.

"It was in the Rue Saint Honore area," replied Jacques.

I remembered Claude mentioning that name when we had gone for dinner, but I was not about to divulge anything in case I incriminated myself.

"What would Claude be doing there?" muttered Monica, more to herself than to us.

"There's a couple of restaurants and clubs in the area," continued Jacques, "so maybe he'd been there."

Should I say something about our dinner date? I surreptitiously removed the restaurant's business card from my jacket pocket and read it. The name of the street was Rue de l'Arbre Sec, which was different from the name that Jacques had used.

"Is Rue de l'Arbre Sec anywhere near where he was arrested?" I asked, reading from the business card.

All three looked at me with surprise.

"How would you know that name?" asked Monica.

"Claude and I went for dinner last night to a restaurant in that street," I said, showing Monica the restaurant's business card.

Jacques looked suspiciously at me while Angelo moved to Monica's side to read the card as well.

"Where exactly were you, Jacques?" questioned Monica.

He suddenly looked sheepish and I wondered if he was in fact telling the truth.

"Well?" asked Monica, again.

At that, Jacques turned and headed out of the office. The three of us sat there bewildered by his reaction and wondering what we should do.

"Do you think he's telling the truth about Claude?" I asked. "Claude had a drink with me last night than suggested we go for dinner, which we did, but there was never any indication or suggestion of drugs of any sort. In fact, the topic of taking drugs never even was raised. I cannot believe that he is into drugs at all. I think Jacques knows something else or Jacques is involved in some way with Claude."

"I really don't believe that there's anything funny going on between them," suggested Monica. "I've known Claude for years and although he does like the boys, he's never ventured into drugs."

"Maybe it's something to do with his boys then?" Suggested Angelo.

"Well, he's never had problems before," continued Monica, shaking her head in disbelief.

I was surprised by the way that Monica spoke about Claude's 'boy', knowing that he was married, but this did not seem to worry her at all.

"I know there's a sauna nearby the restaurant you went to, Nathan," said Angelo, after some thought, "maybe something happened there, if he went to it."

My ears pricked up at the mention of the word sauna, as I thought if I wanted to venture into one, at least I now knew where one was situated and I could get more details from Angelo when Monica was not around.

Just then, the telephone in the office rang. Monica answered the call and we were surprised to hear her mention Claude's name.

"Where are you, mon cher? We are worried about you… we heard that you had been arrested…. Where are you?"

We tried to listen in but could not hear what Claude was saying. Monica continued her conversation with Claude and then replaced the telephone receiver.

"He says he'll be here in an hour. He wouldn't give me too much information but it appears he was taken to a police station but he wouldn't elaborate."

"Do we start without him?" I asked. "Or do we wait for him?"

"You and I can get on with polishing our copy of the script and Angelo, you can finalize your graphics for Claude to see," said Monica, taking charge of the situation.

Angelo headed off to his office, while Monica and I set to work on our copy writing. Almost to the minute, one hour later, Claude came into our office.

"What happened?" asked Monica, hugging him to her.

"It's a long story, but at least I'm out of that horrendous place," said Claude, showing a little embarrassment, as I was his guest and visitor.

"Everything's under control, Claude. Angelo is busy with his graphics and Nathan and I were finalizing our copy for the advert," said Monica, like the ever-reliable assistant.

"Thank you, Monica. Nathan, could I see you in my office for a moment, please?"

I stood up and followed Claude out of our office and into his.

"Please, have a seat."

I sat down opposite from Claude, who looked shaken and almost bewildered by whatever he had been through.

"Nathan, I would rather speak to you about this than any of my staff; for two reasons, namely you'll be going back to the US and I won't have to face you every day with this guilt and second, I couldn't tell my staff and still face them on a daily basis."

I sat intently listening to what Claude wanted to tell me.

"After I dropped you back at your hotel, and I thank you again for the lovely evening we had; I decided to go for another drink near where we had dinner. As I was leaving, and I know I had a bit too much to drink, I saw someone coming out of the sauna nearby and decided to make a move on the person. I saw the young man walk down a dark alley and I followed. There was very little light coming from the other streets and when I neared the person, I could make out the silhouette leaning against the alley wall. I moved up close but still could not make out his features. I felt the front of his jeans that he was wearing and then unzipped them. I sank to my knees on the cobbled street and began to suck his dick. I gradually felt him getting hard and soon my mouth was sliding effortlessly up and down his hard cock.

While I was doing that I sensed another person nearing us, but I kept on working on the person's cock. Suddenly a torch was switched on and the whole alley seemed illuminated."

"Who was it? I mean who had the torch?"

"A gendarme - the police. I looked up and saw who I was sucking; it was Jacques!"

"Our Jacques?" I exclaimed in disbelief.

"Yes, but it doesn't end there. Jacques immediately started shouting that I was abusing him, although he was thoroughly enjoying what I was doing to him. He pushed me away as though he didn't want me sucking him and pleaded with the police that he was innocent and that I had forced myself on him, which of course wasn't true."

"And then…?" I asked, as Claude had gone silent momentarily.

"He kept saying that I had grabbed him and forced myself on him and that he was an innocent victim…. The police arrested me and let him go…"

I was dumbstruck by Jacques behavior and could not understand why he would do something like that, especially when he would have seen it was Claude.

"Did the police lock you up?" I asked, wanting to know more.

"They interrogated me for quite a while and then told me I had to appear in court."

"Had Jacques laid charges against you?"

"No, and that was why I challenged them, asking why I had to appear in court when the so called victim hadn't laid any charges. They said it was public indecency, but then I asked, if that was the case, the victim was also guilty of public indecency and why was he allowed to go free. I think they realized that they were in the wrong, so they let me go with a warning."

I really felt sorry for Claude and what he had been through. He then asked me not to mention any of our conversation to the others, to which I agreed. After our chat, he and I went back to the office where Monica and Angelo were waiting.

"Are we about ready to shoot?" enquired Claude, casually.

"I am and Angelo is, but where's our cameraman?" asked Monica.

"Angelo, do you think you could act as cameraman for the shoot?" requested Claude.

Angelo agreed and so the four of us set off for our journey out of the center of Paris to a farm that Claude knew of out in the country. No one mentioned Claude's previous events during the drive to the countryside, but spoke of other things like the beauty as we passed rivers and farms and open spaces. No mention was made of Claude's experience, but there definitely was a tension in the air during the filming of the advert. I could see how hard Claude was trying to focus on the work at hand and I respected his professionalism. The rest of us supported him throughout the filming.

Being out of the hustle and bustle of central Paris was uplifting not only for me but I think for Claude as well. To be in the open, having lush trees and a river nearby made me forget all the troubles that Claude had gone through. I even saw Monica and Angelo laughing and throwing their weight behind Claude's efforts to succeed with the advert.

After a day of shooting scenes, we headed back to central Paris and the office. Back in the office, Monica asked Claude if she could take him out for dinner. I thought of reciprocating from the previous evening, but I felt that perhaps it would be better for Claude and Monica to spend time together, although I thought it odd that they never considered Claude's wife in the dinner party. Then I realized that if they invited her along, Monica would not have been able to discuss Claude's problem with Jacques, as his wife would ask questions about his whereabouts. Instead, I decided I'd go out that evening to the sauna which was situated near to the restaurant Claude and I had frequented the night before.

We packaged our work away and each of us then left to go our various ways. I gave Claude a hug and told him not to dwell on the previous evening's events too much, meaning his situation with Jacques, and then I got a cab back to my hotel, where I showered and changed into a pair of jeans and a T-shirt. From the hotel, I went out for a bite to eat and then headed in the direction of where I knew the sauna was situated.

CHAPTER 6

Having paid and entered the slightly darkened sauna, I found the lockers and began to undress. A number of other men were busy undressing and I assumed that this was becoming the 'busy' time for this particular sauna. As this was my first visit to the sauna, I was not sure where everything was situated but I was not going to let my lack of direction get in the way of my enjoyment. I followed a couple of the men who had undressed to see where they went and soon I was finding places like the steam room, the dry sauna and a darkened maze with cubicles. In some of the cubicles, I could see, once my eyes had become accustomed to the dim light, a number of men lying on beds in the cubicles. Some appeared to be 'sleeping' while others were stroking their dicks in the hope that a passerby might be interested and enter the cubicle. I wandered around finding my way and then, once I knew where things were situated, headed off to the steam room. I personally prefer steam rooms as saunas tend to dry me out, whereas the steam seems to moisten my body. I entered and closed the glass door behind me. I walked slowly into the room, as it was dark, except for the light coming through the glass door. As I progressed, I accidentally bumped into people, apologizing as I did so. I found a tiled ledge on which one could sit, so I did so and leaned back to luxuriate in the warmth and steam. As my eyes grew used to the limited light, I saw that I was sitting next to someone. From his silhouette, I could see he was probably taller than me and he looked bulkier than me, without looking obese or overweight; his body appeared more muscular. As I sat, feeling the sweat trickle over my body, I felt a hand touch the side of my leg. It was from the silhouetted man next to me. I never removed my leg, as I was there to enjoy myself and have some fun. As I never moved away, my neighbor realized that I would be interested so his hand slid up onto my thigh. Just feeling his touch had immediately aroused me. I knew my dick was getting harder and rising. My neighbor's hand slid towards my inner thigh and soon his fingertips were caressing my moist balls. It felt great and I gave out a sigh as he touched them. His fingers then trailed up over them and wrapped themselves around the swollen shaft of my dick, and he squeezed. My sigh became a low moan. I saw other silhouettes moving in the steam room, moving closer to where the moan had emanated from. Soon there were other hands moving over my sweaty body, and then a mouth clamped around the head of my dick while some others, grabbed my nipples and played with them, flicking and pinching them. My moans had suddenly become louder groans as I received all this attention. I saw my neighbor's face near mine and then felt his lips on mine. He grabbed the back of my head and pulled our lips harder together. His tongue almost leapt into my mouth and I welcomed it as my own tongue playing with his. As we kissed, I could feel and hear his heavy breathing. Someone was busy sucking his dick at the same time as I was receiving the same treatment. He released his mouth from mine and said something in French, which I did not understand.

I whispered back, "Let's go to a cubicle."

I stood up, pushing my cocksucker away, and headed for the steam room door. As I opened the door and exited, I turned to see if my neighbor was following. Sure enough, the tall, muscular figure was behind me. With our towels wrapped around our waists and with protruding dicks tenting the towels, we headed in the direction of the cubicles. On finding an empty on, I entered, followed closely by my neighbor. I dropped my towel on the floor and lay on the bed. My neighbor did likewise and lowered his body on top of mine.

His mouth found mine again and soon our dicks were rubbing together and our moans and groans were reverberating around the cubicle. In between the groans and the odd French phrases, that left his lips, my neighbor's mouth remained plastered to mine and I could feel his powerful chest squashing me as he continued to writhe over my body. Our passion continued until I could not withhold his weight on me anymore, so I tried to wriggle free. Although he did not want me to break free, he realized how worked-up we had both become.

"Must have a cigarette," he said in broken English.

He had a small plastic bag in which were some cigarettes and a lighter. He obviously carried these around with him in the plastic so that when he went into the steam room, they would not get soaked. As he clicked the lighter to light his cigarette, I saw in the glow of the flame, his facial and bodily features. A slight gasp came from me as he looked about fifty years old, with gray hair and a well-built body of someone who has spent most of his life visiting the gym and continues to do so. Immediately I wanted to drop to my knees and worship this Daddy. His long, thick cock was bobbing and I could see how his foreskin had been pulled right back to reveal a thickly rounded cock head, just waiting for my mouth to encompass it. He lay back, puffing on his cigarette while I knelt between his muscular thighs and sucked on that broad glistening cock head. Now that I knew what he looked like, I was more passionate and more determined to get this Daddy to fuck my ass for me. My mouth worked up and down the full length of his cock while he relaxed with his cigarette. As I began to work him up, he stubbed out his cigarette and, grabbing me by the arms, rolled me over onto my back and reciprocated what I had been doing to him.

"You are beautiful," he groaned in between mouthfuls of my cock.

"Daddy, push that cock of yours deep into my ass," I pleaded, as his mouth sank to the base of my cock and his chin brushed my balls.

His hands ran over my nipples, brushing over them roughly, causing me to thrust my hips up and forcing my cock deeper down his throat. He never gagged but enjoyed the extra thrust. Again, I pleaded with him to ravage my ass as he was getting me closer to shooting, but he still ignored me and continued to suck on both my cock and my balls, pushing me higher and higher to my climax. He leant in to me and I grabbed his nipples, which I tweaked and pinched. The harder I pinched, the more he groaned and the harder he sucked on my cock. I realized that he liked his nipples being pinched so I ground them in between my fingertips. He suddenly released the grip on my cock and nipples and hoisted my legs skywards. There was no gentleness in his actions and grabbing hold of the shaft of his thick cock, he rammed it into my ass. The sudden pain was intense and I cried out as he sank it into my asshole. His attack took the wind out of me and I was gasping for air as he sank deeper into my tight hole. When he could go no further, he withdrew with the same intensity and rammed it back in. He kept this up for some time, thrusting in and out and making my body shudder with each attack. Slowly I was becoming used to his size and intensity and was beginning to enjoy the roughness of his actions and was thrusting back to meet each of his thrusts until both our bodies were rocking back and forth. I clamped my fingers back onto his nipples and squeezed hard. A deep growl was emitted from his throat and his thrusts became more frantic.

"Fuck me Daddy! Fuck me harder, Daddy!" I cried out.

I did not have to tell him what to do or what I wanted; he knew and he was determined to give me everything we both wanted. His grunts as he thrust became louder and both of us were sweating profusely from the action. His cock was sliding in and out of my ass with ease now and each time he pushed in, he would slap his thighs against my ass cheeks. I was getting closer to shooting and again I warned him, but I also did not want him to stop. I wanted this gray-haired Daddy inside of me for much longer, but I knew that was not going to happen as I could feel his cock swelling in me, getting ready to come. I gave a last sharp pinch with my fingers on his nipples and he fired into my body. His gasps were now more like desperate cries and both of us were firing cum all over the cubicle. After his first salvo in my body, he had pulled his cock free and was jerking off and emptying his load all over my stomach and chest, while mine was spraying both of us. The groans and moans seemed to silence the rest of the building, as I heard nothing other than our pleasure being emitted. Our breathing was heavy and the sweat from both of us was intermingling.

As he slowly began to come off his high, he lowered his muscular body onto mine and smeared our cum with his chest and stomach, then he slid off of me and lay next to me on the bed in the cubicle, our breathing slowly resuming normality.

"You are a good fuck," he said in between gasps.

"No, Daddy, you're the good fuck."

I did not say it, but I was so impressed with this man's ability to perform like he did, especially considering his imagined age. I had been with younger guys who couldn't match the stamina and ability that he had, and added to that was his ability to please me mentally and physically. Again many of the younger guys only want to get off with you and aren't worried how much pleasure they're bringing to you, if any. It is more a case of 'wham bam thank you mam!"

As we lay there, not speaking, he lit up another cigarette, enabling me to view him in the glow once more and admire his physical appearance. I snuggled into his chest and he laid his free arm around me and pulled me closer to him. I had a feeling of safety and love come from him and I was happy to stay like that all night, if need be.

As I lay there, I whispered, "by the way, my name's Nathan."

He grunted an acknowledgement and said, "I'm Claude."

I was happy to be in Claude's care but I wondered how he had felt about the whole session that we had had.

"You want something to drink?" asked Claude.

"That would be nice," I replied, knowing that we would not just get up and disappear into the darkness, and that there was the hope we might exchange addresses at least.

When he had finished his cigarette, we got off the bed, wrapped our towels around us and went to have something to drink at the sauna's bar. In the light of the bar, I was able to see all Claude's finer features. Although his face was rugged like someone who had spent most of their life outdoors, he was handsome and I could see now how well defined his body was. As I stared at his beautiful physique, I could not resist saying, "You must be very popular with the guys here, Claude."

He smiled and shook his head as if to say that he was not.

"You're so good looking and have such a fine body – not to mention what you've got between your legs," I said, returning the smile.

He laughed out aloud at my comment.

"You are so sweet, Nathan. Not many guys of your age are interested in older men like me. There are a few but most of the younger guys want to be with men their own age."

"Well I prefer older guys," I added. "I think they have more maturity and they know what to do to please a guy, like you did."

Claude was flattered by my comment and squeezed my thigh as we sat together.

"Do you have a boyfriend?" he asked, his hand still resting on my thigh.

"No. Do you?"

"I don't have a steady boyfriend, but I have a few boys who like me to service them."

'Service' was the right word. That is exactly what Claude had done for me and he knew how to do it well.

"I bet those boys are lining up to be serviced by you," I continued, with a smile

Claude merely shrugged his shoulders and laughed.

"Let us say I don't have to go looking for guys when I want sex, but don't misunderstand me when I say that. I don't go out every day."

This time it was my turn to laugh. I could fully understand that Claude could have a different person every day if he so wished, with his good looks and serious sex appeal.

"Are you on holiday here in Paris?" enquired Claude.

"No. Actually I'm here for about a week at the most on business."

"Oh, that's a pity, because I would like to have spent more time with you. You seem an interesting person."

"Thanks for the compliment, but I'm here to do an advert and then it's back to the US."

"Ah, you are an actor then?" asked Claude, his face lighting up as though he thought I might be a superstar.

"Nothing as grand as that Claude; I'm in the advertising trade and I'm just a copywriter."

His face dropped a little, but the smile was still there.

"No problem. You are still interesting to me. Do you know any people here in Paris?"

"I was given the name and number of one of the flight stewards on the plane when I came over. His name is Pierre and he stays here in Paris with a friend called Marcel who apparently is a photographer."

"Ah," gasped Claude, "I know a Marcel who's a photographer and I do remember meeting a friend of his who said he was a flight steward, but I don't remember his name."

"Do you remember what the friend looked like?" I asked.

"I think he was slim and tall. He had slightly receding hair, if I remember, and was about thirty or a little younger perhaps."

"Sounds like Pierre," I responded"

"If they are the same people that I'm thinking of, then Marcel is one of my boys."

I was not sure how to respond to that, except say "Oh!"

"Very nice young man. He likes to take photos of us fucking."

"How does he do that if you're busy with him?"

"He sets the camera on a timer and then we get into various positions. I've even learnt to use his camera so that when I'm sliding in and out of his ass, I can capture it on camera."

I began to get aroused listening and imagining what was going on between them. I even thought of phoning Pierre and seeing if he was interested in meeting me and perhaps I could persuade him and Marcel to have a threesome with photos included. My mind seemed to dwell on Pierre and Marcel and was not focusing on what Claude was saying, eventually, he tapped me on the leg and asked," Are you with me?"

"Sorry, Claude, my mind was somewhere else."

"I could see that. I asked if you would like to go round to Marcel's apartment. I'm sure he'd be happy to see me and if his friend's there as well, maybe we could have a four-some."

That really got my attention.

"Do you feel like going there?" I asked, hoping that Claude would make my decision for me. If he said 'yes' then I'd go along for the fun, but if he said 'no', then it wouldn't worry me and I'd probably head back to my hotel.

"Come on, let's get dressed and go there," he said.

We went to the change room and dressed then got into Claude's car, which was parked around the corner from the sauna, and were soon heading through the streets of Paris on our way to Pierre and Marcel's apartment.

CHAPTER 7

"It's Claude here," he said after buzzing Marcel's apartment.

The door to the old building opened and we both entered and got the rickety elevator up to the seventh floor. We emerged from the elevator and headed down a long corridor. We soon found ourselves outside apartment number 705. Claude rang the doorbell. The door was opened by a young man in what I thought was his early twenties. He had dark hair and a goatee. He had dark eyes but they twinkled when he saw Claude.

"Bon soir, mon amour!" said Claude, flinging his arms around the young man. "Marcel, let me introduce you to a new friend. This is Nathan, from America."

Marcel extended a hand to shake mine and said, "You are most welcome."

He ushered us into his neatly furnished apartment and almost on cue, the voice of Pierre rang out, asking something in French.

Marcel replied to him and then Pierre appeared. As he saw me, he rushed over and flung his arms around me, hugging me tightly.

"What are you doing here?" asked Pierre, excitedly.

"It was Claude's idea to come and visit you in the middle of the night. I'm sorry I couldn't phone to warn you, but, here we are."

"Come in, come in!" said Pierre closing the front door behind us.

As I looked at Pierre and Marcel, it appeared to me that Pierre was probably the older of the two. We made ourselves comfortable in their lounge and Marcel rushed off to the kitchen to make coffee for Pierre and myself and get drinks for him and Claude. Pierre was extremely excited to see me again and wanted to know how I was enjoying Paris.

"Well, I haven't really had much time to see the sights as I've been working all day and it's only in the evenings that I've been free," I answered.

"Where did you two meet?" asked Marcel, emerging from the kitchen carrying the drinks for him and Claude. "The coffee is on the boil," he added.

"I met Nathan at the sauna," said Claude, almost proudly as though I was some special person.

"And what were you doing there?" asked Pierre, "looking for some Frenchmen?"

"Of course," I joked, "And I found one," I continued, pointing to Claude.

"I've been thinking about you," said Marcel, to Claude. "I was wondering where you had got to."

"Well, I've been around," replied Claude. "Why didn't you call?"

Marcel merely shrugged. However, I sensed that he was extremely happy to see Claude again and I noticed how his attitude changed towards the group. Marcel paid little attention to Pierre, or me and began to sidle up to Claude. It was not long before Marcel had dragged Claude off to the main bedroom where Pierre and I could clearly hear their whisperings and moans that had surfaced.

"Sounds as if things are hotting up in there," said Pierre, almost blushing.

I looked at Pierre and then thought of Claude with Marcel. Dare I suggest that we join them, or should I make a move on Pierre? I noticed Pierre place a hand on his crotch as the sounds built up louder from the bedroom. I was beginning to think that Pierre was eager to join in the action that was taking place in the main bedroom; as he stood up and walked slightly closer to the open doorway to peer in. As he stood there with his back to me, I could see from the movement of his right arm, that he was rubbing his hand over his crotch. I quietly rose from my seat, moved to behind Pierre, and looked over his shoulder into the room.

A naked Marcel was between Claude's spread legs and was sucking on Claude's cock. I wrapped my arms around Pierre's waist and let my right hand drift to his crotch area. I felt his hard cock and squeezed it. Instantly he gave out a sigh that alerted Marcel, who turned to see who was there. On seeing both of us there, he motioned with his free hand to join them. His other hand was busy massaging Claude's balls for him.

In the blink of an eye, both Pierre and I were naked and on the bed, Pierre feeding his long cock into Claude's mouth while I began to rim Marcel's ass as he bent over Claude's cock, deep down his throat. I could hear Marcel's groans as I worked on his ass and I knew that Pierre was being treated well by Claude, who could take any size dick down his throat.

Marcel released his grip on Claude's cock and muttered to him and me, "I want you both to fuck me, please Daddies."

I was surprised to be classified in the 'Daddy' category along with Claude. If anyone was a Daddy, it was Claude. He had the age, the mature well-built body and the looks to be a Daddy, but when an ass was being offered to me like this, who was I to turn down an offer? I pushed Marcel forward so that his ass hovered over Claude's massive, wet cock and I watched with awe as Marcel sank down onto it without so much as a flinch or a cry. This boy was used to Claude's size and he knew how to use his ass on the thick rod that was penetrating his fine ass. Marcel rode Claude's cock for some time, bouncing up and down and then he turned to me and said, "Fuck me Daddy!"

I pushed him forward so that he was now kissing Claude. By doing this, it opened up his ass for me to slide in alongside of Claude's cock. I took hold of my hard shaft, aimed it at his pulsating ass, and pushed forward. Even as I sank into the warmth of his ass and felt Claude's cock pushing against mine, Marcel still did not whimper, cry or complain. Claude was the one moaning as he felt my cock slide along his thick shaft. Once I was embedded in Marcel's ass, I began to thrust deeper and at the same time, Claude began upward thrusts into Marcel's ass. As the two of us began fucking his ass, so Marcel now began to cry out and ask both of us to fuck him harder and deeper. We obliged and the more we obliged, the more Marcel became excited and rode us like someone riding a bucking bronco. All this time, Pierre had continued to feed Claude his dripping wet cock until he could not take it anymore and fired his load into Claude's throat. My Daddy friend swallowed and gulped as the load sped down his throat, but he never let go of Pierre's cock until he had drained it of every drop of cum.

From the constant friction of Claude's cock against mine, I knew that I would probably be the next to shoot. I was right. I cried out that I was about to cum and immediately Marcel became even more robust on our cocks and I thought mine might slip out of its enclosure, but I pushed harder and then I felt my balls rise up and the first salvo of cum sped into his chute. I cried and groaned as I released my load and Marcel made sure that he drained every drop from me by clenching his ass and squeezing my cock shaft.

As I slipped from the grasp of his tight ass muscles, so Claude growled and fired into Marcel. While he did this, both Pierre and I jerked Marcel's cock and sucked its wet head, bringing the boy to his climax. My mouth was covering his cock head as he fired and Pierre continued jerking him off as load after load flew into my mouth and I hurriedly swallowed. As the last drops were drained from Marcel, I let his limp cock slip from my mouth and at the same time, Marcel sighed.

"Thank you Daddies, you were both great. Now I really feel fucked," he said, slowly lifting his ass off Claude's still hard cock and collapsing onto the bed, breathing heavily. As for the rest of us, we all relaxed alongside Marcel, our hands caressing each other until we dozed off to sleep.

In the early hours of the morning, I awoke to the sounds of grunting. I opened my eyes and found Claude and Pierre busy in a sixty-nine position, sucking each other's cocks. I lay and watched in the dim light that emerged from the streetlights below and the glow of a full moon. I could feel myself becoming aroused once more and wondered if I should join in or just watch. This time I decided to be the voyeur. I glanced around and saw that Marcel was missing, so I presumed he had gone through to the other bedroom at some stage in the night. I lay naked on the top of the bed as the other two engrossed themselves in each other. My cock was full-blown and hard as I watched them, but I chose not to stroke my shaft. Instead, I rubbed the palm of my hand over my cock head, enjoying the warmth I created with this gentle action.

Claude rolled Pierre onto his back and hoisted his legs high into the air. While he held them up, he sucked on Pierre's asshole and began to rim it with his tongue. Pierre's groans became audible now and I knew that he was enjoying Claude's touches. Claude's tongue was slurping loudly over the pulsating hole and then he licked his way up towards Pierre's balls, opening his mouth as wide as he could and sucking both orbs into his mouth at the same time. Pierre gave a quaint cry of delight as both balls got sucked into Claude's mouth and he began to suck on them and roll his tongue over them. By now, Claude had inserted a finger that was grinding in Pierre's ass, causing him to groan and coo with pleasure.

"*Fuck me, please,*" moaned Pierre in French, but Claude continued to suck on the air steward's balls while his finger massaged the inner passage of his ass.

Pierre was now writhing on the finger that was going deeper into his chute, and cooing more loudly. I was rock hard as I listened and watched the two men. I was becoming desperate to join in, but was not sure if I would be breaking into something private and special between the two men. I turned, as if in my sleep so that I would be nearer to them and perhaps one of them might see my hard on and do something to show that they wanted me to be part of their action.

Claude's shoulders now held Pierre's legs up high while his mouth continued its work on the thickening, wet cock and one hand manipulated Pierre's asshole. With his other free hand, Claude stretched across to where I was and took hold of my solid, hard cock. It felt good to have been included in their action and although I gave the air of being half-asleep, I was more than willing to get involved. I manipulated myself into a position so that my face was near Claude's ass and as I burrowed to get under it, he raised his ass to give me easier access. My tongue shot out and lathered his crack, searching for his pucker, which I soon found. As my tongue darted into Claude's ass, I felt it clamp onto my tongue as if to prevent me access, but I pushed forward and soon my tongue tip was lubricating his hole. In between Claude's sucking sounds, he included some groans as my tongue washed his ass. With my hands, I spread his ass cheeks, opening up his ass wider and then I included my fingers so both fingers and tongue began to explore his ass. I felt as he forced his ass back onto my face and found my mouth and nose between his crack. His musky smell made me feel heady and I almost wanted to push my face right into his opening. I realized that the more I worked on Claude's ass, the more frenetic he was with Pierre, getting himself worked up and groaning even louder, until he had to release his grip on Pierre's balls and cock, remove his finger from Pierre's ass and slide his thick, long cock into the depths of the sir steward.

Pierre cried out as he felt the thick, hard rod sink into him. At the same time, my fingers began to delve into Claude's ass, driving them deeper and every time that Claude thrust into Pierre's ass, so my fingers did likewise into Claude's ass. With one hand I began to fist-fuck Claude and with the other, I worked over my length, stroking my cock in time to Claude's thrusts. All three of us were now in a state of euphoria as we brought pleasure to each other. The sound of heavy breathing, groans, grunts and expletives, reverberated around the room. No one cared if anyone else heard these sounds so long as we were enjoying the touch of someone else.

Pierre did not take long to roar as he fired onto Claude's face that had neared his erupting cock. A stream of white cum splashed across Claude's face, quickly followed by another stream. Each time, Pierre's ass clamped tightly onto Claude's shaft, strangling it and tightening his grip on the thick cock that was pounding faster and faster. I drove my fingers in deep, spreading them as I did so and causing Claude to cry out as he felt the expansion in his chute. I quickly adjusted my position so that when I was ready to come, I would shoot onto Claude's asshole. Claude growled loudly, pushed back onto my fingers and then almost flung his cock back deeply into Pierre's ass. I knew he was coming as I felt the way his asshole clamped around my fingers; I stroked my cock furiously to try to come at the same time as Claude. As I knew his load was firing from the tip of his massive cock, so I emptied my load into the opening of his ass. My cum splashed onto my fingers making them more slippery as they slid in and out of his ass and I continued massaging his asshole while I continued to splay my juices over Claude's ass.

As my fingers emerged from Claude's warm ass, so he fell forwards onto Pierre's body and their lips met and Pierre began to lick off some of the cum that was still covering Claude's face, while I did likewise on Claude's ass. When we had cleaned each other, we lay together and drifted off to sleep again.

CHAPTER 8

When I arrived at work the following morning, unexpectedly late, after my hectic night, Claude looked askance at me and I knew he was wondering why I was late and therefore what I had been doing the night before. I was not about to divulge my previous evening's escapades in front of the others, so I merely apologized and took my seat around the boardroom table.

Claude explained what was planned for today and said that while he and Angelo were busy editing the film from the previous day, he wanted Monica and me to do the editing of the dialogue.

Monica could see I was bit 'under the weather', so she took charge and did most of the work.

"Bad night last night, Nathan?" she asked at one stage as I gave a long, drawn-out yawn.

"I suppose you could say that," I answered, without giving anything away.

"Well, so long as you enjoyed it," replied Monica, with a glint in her eye.

I smiled back and nodded. Enough said! She understood.

Once we had completed our part of the work, we reported to Claude who was also in the final stages of their editing. Later that afternoon, the advert was completed and I realized that my work in Paris was over.

"When will you be leaving?" asked Claude.

"Well, that's up to you. If you're happy that everything's finished, then I suppose I'll probably fly back tomorrow."

I could see from his facial expression that he was not happy to see me go so soon, but I had no other reason to stay in Paris.

"It would be lovely if you could stay a few more days," said Claude, with an almost pleading, puppy dog look on his face.

I felt for him, particularly after his predicament with Jacques.

"Have you heard anything more about Jacques?" I enquired, wondering if the young man had returned to the office.

Claude looked somewhat embarrassed and tried to avoid the question.

"Has he made contact with you?" I persevered.

Again, Claude tried to push the conversation in another direction, but I was going to be persistent.

"He has contacted you, hasn't he?"

Finally, Claude, realizing that I was not going to give up my line of questioning, answered.

"Yes, he did phone me."

"And?"

Claude hesitated.

"He came round to my apartment last night."

"By himself?"

"Yes."

"And?"

"Well we spoke," said Claude, rather hesitantly.

"So what did he say?"

"He apologized for the trouble he had caused."

"Is that all? Did he say why he'd done that to you?"

Once more, there was the element of hesitation from Claude. I was sensing that something must have happened and he was embarrassed to tell. After much hesitation, I decided to be direct with Claude.

"Did he spend the night with you?"

Claude blushed but never responded to my question.

"Claude, you let him spend the night with you after what he did to you, didn't you."

"Yes, but it's not like you think it is."

"Oh and what do I think it is?"

"You think we had sex, I suppose."

"Well you did, didn't you? I bet Jacques pleaded with you and you know how he would have wanted his daddy to fuck him and how desperate you would have been to oblige, so you did."

Claude hung his head almost in shame. He could not face me, especially as we had all stood behind him after his debacle with the police, and now he had welcomed his 'attacker' into his home again.

"Claude those are your choices. I would have thought after what he had done to you, that you wouldn't have anything to do with him again, but who am I to judge?"

"I'm sorry, Nathan. It is just that I feel for the young boy. I do like him and I know he likes me."

"If he liked you so much, as you say, why did he turn on you and basically hand you over to the police. Someone who loves or likes someone else doesn't do that sort of thing – well certainly not in my estimation."

"I know that I'm probably wrong in what I did, but then so was he wrong, but feelings go deeper, you know. I am his Daddy and he is my boy and just like any other young boy, they all make mistakes. When you were young I'm sure you made similar mistakes."

"Claude, I'm still young and I certainly try not to make the sort of mistakes that Jacques made, as you put it. Yes, I agree that no one is perfect, but to turn on a friend is unacceptable."

I listened to myself saying these things and wondered where they were coming from. Sure, I was still young, but there was a sense of maturity in me and I wondered if at this young age I was becoming like a real Daddy with maturity and sex appeal, but without the silver-gray hair. I wondered what Uncle Cecil would have said had he been with me in Paris to hear these conversations. Claude continued on his explanation as to why he had welcomed Jacques back into his apartment, but I was not really paying much attention to what he was saying. My thoughts were going back to Uncle Cecil and Frank and wondering how they were.

I suddenly turned to Claude.

"I think if we've done everything that has to be done here, that I'm going to try to get a flight back tomorrow."

I had enjoyed Paris, but as language was an issue here, I wanted to get home where everyone understood English and I could communicate much better and easier.

From the office, I telephoned the airline to see if I could get a seat on a flight. I was lucky and having been assured of a seat, I set about saying my goodbyes to those I had made acquaintance in Paris.

Claude was obviously sorry to see me go and so was Monica. Angelo had not had much to do with me and we had not connected so saying goodbye to him was not that daunting.

On the day of my departure, I showered, dressed and called a cab to take me to Charles de Gaulle airport where I caught my flight back to Miami and then get the connection to Fort Lauderdale.

I had phoned Uncle Cecil, but only got the answering machine. I had left a message but still did not know if he would be at the airport to meet me.

When I landed at the airport, I was surprised to see Frank there but no Uncle Cecil. Frank flung his arms around me like some long, lost child.

"Where's Uncle Cecil?" I asked, trying to gather my breath from his bear hug.

"He's busy and he asked me to fetch you. I hope you didn't mind?"

"Mind!" I exclaimed. I was ecstatic to see Frank.

In one week, or less, I had missed both him and Uncle Cecil. Although I had met other people, I still yearned to be back home with those I was closest to.

"I'm taking you back to my place and Cecil said that he would join us for lunch. How are you feeling after the long flight?"

"Fine, thanks. I'm lucky that I can sleep on planes, so I'm not jet-lagged or tired," I replied.

"Good, as I have to stop off and pick up some food for us on the way home."

We threw my bags into the trunk of Frank's car and headed off to his place.

"Well, how was Paris, or should I say, how were the men?" enquired Frank, with a sense of excitement in his voice.

"Paris was lovely," I answered, but never mentioned the men, just to tease him.

"Sure, sure! But what about the men?" he persisted.

"Oh, I suppose they weren't too bad," I continued nonchalantly.

I could see that he was becoming agitated by my answers.

"Come on boy, spill the stories. I know with your looks and that fine body, you'd have picked up any number of men."

"Well, that's where you're wrong. I was celibate."

"Celibate!" exploded Frank. "You can't even spell the word let alone know what it means."

"Ok, ok! I had a few."

"Oh, he had a few," said Frank, mimicking my answer. "Were you a good boy?"

I smiled and nodded. Then I added, "And I was a good daddy."

Frank's eyes widened.

"A daddy!"

"Sure, does that surprise you?"

"I've always said to Cecil that one day you'll make an awesome daddy for some boy. So tell me more."

I proceeded to tell Frank about Claude and the first day there, and then I told him about my meeting in the sauna with Claude and finally treating Marcel and Pierre to a taste of good old American cock. He seemed most impressed, and throughout my telling him of my trip, I noticed how he played with his crotch, squeezing it every time I mentioned the act of having sex. I was making Frank horny.

When we arrived at his apartment, he unloaded my luggage and the two of us caught the elevator up to his apartment. Once we were inside, he dropped my bags and once again grabbed me, hugging me to him, and as he did so, I could feel his thick cock getting harder and pressing against my stomach. I must admit I was a bit surprised by Frank's passionate welcome. It was not what I expected as we only recently had got to know each other. I reciprocated by hugging him as well, but he seemed not to want to let go. Eventually he dropped the hugs and offered me something to drink.

"Coffee if you don't mind, Frank."

"Come through to the kitchen and tell me all about your trip," he said, exiting the lounge and rushing into the tidy kitchen.

I followed like the inevitable sheep and proceeded to tell Frank as much of my trip as I wanted him to know. I never mentioned the attack on Claude and didn't fill Frank into the details of Claude, Pierre and Marcel, although I was tempted to tell him, as I was proud of my 'Daddy' role in our foursome.

"So what have you guys been up to since I was away?"

Frank was not too forthcoming with what I thought they might have been up to, but he did tell me that he and Uncle Cecil had been for a drink one night and a fight had broken out, but neither of them was involved in it – thank goodness!

"I know your Uncle Cecil had a date the other night, but I'm not sure what happened as he's not saying a word to me about it. Either he's met someone special, or it was a total flop."

"I'll see if I can get something out of him," I quipped, laughing as I said it.

We finished our coffee just as the front doorbell rang.

"I bet that's Cecil," said Frank rising and going to the door.

"Welcome," said Frank as he opened the door. "It's about time you arrived."

"Is our boy here?" asked Uncle Cecil.

When he entered the lounge and saw me, he too flung his arms around me as though I had been away for a year at least.

"How are you my boy?" asked Uncle Cecil, giving me a kiss on the cheek as he hugged me.

"I'm fine thanks and I had a great time, although it was short. But, how are you?"

"I'm well, thanks."

"I believe you've been having a good time while I've been away," I added.

Uncle Cecil looked a little surprised by my statement and blushed.

"I see from the color of your face, you've been up to mischief," I continued.

"Frank! Have you been spreading rumors?" enquired Uncle Cecil, in a rather reprimanding manner.

"Not at all, have I, Nathan?"

"Of course not, but news does travel, even if it is overseas."

"I've done nothing to bring shame on the family," retorted Uncle Cecil.

"But you've been up to no good, haven't you?" I asked, raising an eyebrow as I said it in a questioning manner.

Uncle Cecil merely sniggered.

"Frank *has* been saying something, hasn't he?"

"My old friend, I haven't said a word because I don't know what you did on your date. You still haven't told me."

"And I'm not about to divulge what happened, either. Now tell me all about Paris."

I regaled Uncle Cecil with my adventures, much along the same lines as I had told Frank, but was not interrogated about bits that I might have left out or Uncle Cecil found intriguing.

"While I get us something to drink, you two get chatting," said Frank, hurrying back into the kitchen.

"While he's out of earshot, I have to tell you that I think he's missed you, Nathan. From the time you left, he has been nagging me for news of you and on one occasion, he even said he hoped that you did not flaunt your body with any other guys. Sounds a little jealous to me."

"Wow! Sounds like it. I never thought he was that interested in me."

"But, I must tell you that I think he's going to proposition you about something," added Uncle Cecil.

"Uncle Cecil, proposition is such an old fashioned word. Are you meaning what I think you mean?"

"I don't know what you mean, but I know he said that he wanted to talk seriously to you, and seriously to me means that he wants to have some sort of relationship with you."

Just then, Frank reappeared from the kitchen carrying a tray with drinks and some snacks on it.

"Sustenance for everyone," said Frank, placing the tray on the low coffee table.

He handed us our drinks and then offered a plate of snacks to us. Uncle Cecil took two delicate hors d'oeuvres, but as I had eaten on the plane, I politely refused the food. The three of us settled down to idle chatter and soon Frank mentioned that he needed to speak to me about something, but did not elaborate on the topic. I caught Uncle Cecil glance in my direction and wink, knowingly, but the mention of the topic was raised and then dropped. As I sat sipping my drink, a cold beer, I took the opportunity to caste a glance at Frank, wondering whether he was going to 'propose' to me in some way. It had not crossed my mind before, but now that Uncle Cecil had made mention of the possibility of something romantic happening, I looked long and hard at Frank. He certainly had aged well; was still good-looking; had himself a good, well-kept body and certainly knew how to make love. Mentally I began to tick the relevant boxes relating to his qualities. Looks – yes; body – yes; cock – YES; they all seemed in order, but I didn't know what his temperament was like as I'd only been with him in a social context. While I was deep in thought of the possible prospect of becoming one of Frank's permanent boys, he interrupted my thoughts.

"Nathan, where are you? Still in Paris?"

"Oh, sorry, Frank. I was miles away; maybe it's the jetlag."

"Rubbish! You would not have jetlag on that flight. I think your thoughts are with the many memories of Paris."

I grinned embarrassedly and asked what he wanted to ask or tell me.

"Nathan, I was wondering if you'd consider doing something for me," said Frank.

Uncle Cecil adjusted himself in his seat, as though he were the expectant mother waiting for a beau to propose to his daughter. He smiled broadly in expectation of some good news.

"I was wondering if you'd assist me in a reality program, Nathan."

"Reality program!" exclaimed an exasperated Uncle Cecil, his face becoming a picture of disillusionment. "What do you mean by that?"

"I was hoping that Nathan could be part of a reality program we're doing about a group of gay men."

I said nothing but watched as the banter went from Frank and then to Uncle Cecil, who was not impressed by the request from Frank.

"You can't expect my boy to cavort around with a group of unknown gay men," continued Uncle Cecil, becoming more and more protective of me. "He's too handsome to be thrown in among such people and in any case, what are you going to pay him"

I laughed as it seemed the obvious thing for Uncle Cecil to think of – money!

"Nothing! I was hoping that he'd do it as a favor to me," said Frank, almost innocently.

"Free!" screamed Uncle Cecil. "Have you gone crazy? This boy is too valuable to be put out into some strange program of yours, and not for free!"

"Cecil, it's actually up to Nathan to decide. He's not a baby anymore and besides, he's not your son."

Silence fell over the room and I could see that Uncle Cecil was not impressed by Frank's proposition. I envisaged working with Frank might be exciting, but I did not want to upset either man.

"What does it entail?" I asked Frank.

"Well, without giving too much away, it's a group of young gay men who are going to live together and each week one will be eliminated until we have a winner."

Uncle Cecil's face was a picture of horror as each word came out of Frank's mouth. Then once he heard the word 'winner', he became more interested.

"What's the prize?" enquired an eager Cecil.

"Fifty thousand dollars," replied Frank casually.

Both my and Uncle Cecil's eyes lit up with excitement at eth mention of the prize.

"Now tell me Frank, how well will he be treated?"

"Just the same as the other contestants and we'll be keeping an eye on all of them."

"How many others are there going to be?" I asked Frank.

"Including yourself, there will be nine other guys, making it a total of ten of you."

"And what are these... so called young men ... going to be doing?" asked a rather smug Uncle Cecil.

"Anything they want and of course we will be setting them tasks to complete as well," answered Frank.

"I'm still a little worried," continued Uncle Cecil.

"Cecil, I think you know me well enough to know that I'd never let the boy be in danger. Shit! He means a lot to me," replied Frank.

This was the first time that I had heard Frank say something relating to me in this manner. He had never before said anything about feelings and this came as a complete surprise to me, and probably Uncle Cecil.

"So what is this going to entail?" I enquired.

"Nathan, I'll give you a call when we're ready and I'll explain all the details then," said Frank, giving my shoulder a squeeze with his heavy hand.

CHAPTER 9

It was a rainy Sunday afternoon when Frank contacted me. He sent a car to pick me up and take me round to his apartment where he was waiting with a pot of strong coffee and a few snacks.

"The coffee's to keep you alert and the snacks are to fill that stomach of yours," said Frank, ushering me into his lounge. There were two other young men already seated there drinking coffee.

"Hi, I'm Nathan," I said to both of them.

"I'm Rob," said the tall blonde-haired person, raising a hand to give a half-hearted wave to me.

"And I'm Greg," replied the dark haired guy, who looked about nineteen years old.

I wondered if they were both contestants or whether these were more of Frank's 'acquaintances', but I was not about to ask them. I would wait for Frank to put me in the picture.

"Coffee, Nathan?" asked Frank, automatically pouring me a cup before I had a chance to respond to his question.

"Thanks Frank," I answered, taking the steaming cup from him.

"I see you've got yourself acquainted with Greg and Rob. These are a couple of the guys you'll be competing with. Rob is a manager and Greg is a hairdresser friend of mine who has agreed to take part. The other seven contestants have already been briefed on the program."

I smiled at the two men and gave a slight nod of the head to acknowledge them. Rob appealed to me, but I found Greg too young looking and was not really my type. Maybe he found me attractive, I do not know, but I was not about to make a pass at him at any time.

Rob was slightly muscular without being excessively like a Mr. Universe, while Greg was skinny and looked like the type that Frank would fuck all night and never tire of his actions. Rob had the tiniest of goatees, which made his face look not only manly but also sexy. Although he had blond hair, it was receding slightly in the front and that too added to his macho appeal. From the way he sat, with his legs spread wide, I could see that he carried a hefty bulge in the front of his jeans, while Greg sat 'demurely' with his legs crossed, almost hiding his crotch. The two of them sat on Frank's sofa and Frank and I sat in two easy chairs, facing them.

"Guys, what is going to happen is that you and the other seven guys will be placed in a house together where you'll live for ten weeks. We have arranged sufficient accommodation for all of you and there will be enough food for the first week. After that you guys will have to budget to buy food stuffs and anything else that you need in the house. In between this, you'll have time to relax and get to know each other and as I mentioned to you before, there will be tasks and competitions that you'll have to endure."

We all sat staring at each other, not knowing whether to ask any questions or not.

"Well," asked Frank, "do you have any questions?"

"Um, when does this start?" asked Rob.

"Tomorrow. You will be picked up from your homes and driven to the house where you will meet the others. Once you are there, that is where you will stay until you are eliminated. Oh, and before I forget, once you're in the house there's no going out unless you're eliminated."

"You mean we're like prisoners?" enquired Greg, looking rather bewildered.

"I wouldn't call it that, Greg," said Frank, smiling at Greg to give him a feeling of cool composure. "All it constitutes is a group of young men who all happen to be gay, living together under one roof. I suppose it might be like a fraternity, if you want to look at it in that light."

We all nodded in understanding but we never asked anything more.

"Well, guys, if you have no more questions, you're free to leave," said Frank rising and going to open the front door for us.

As we departed, Rob and I hesitated and waited until Greg had left.

"What do you make of all this, Nathan?"

I chuckled.

"Actually, I think it could be fun, if you know what I mean."

"I suppose it's fun being with a gang of gay guys that you don't know, but how do you think we'll all get along?" asked Rob.

"I think that's a major part of the reality show; to see how we cope together."

"But they're filming this aren't they?"

"Sure," I replied.

"So that means… when we shower…"

I burst out laughing.

"Oh boy! That means the public will see us naked."

We both laughed heartily at the thought of us being naked in the shower for the entire world to see.

"Do you have a problem with that?" asked Rob, smiling broadly at me.

"Not at all. I don't mind being naked at all, but I was thinking, if we're going to share rooms and we have a choice, would you be willing to share with me?"

"I'd like that," replied Rob. "At least we've met and you seem a decent sort of guy."

"Gee thanks, so are you," I reciprocated.

I was very happy to know that he was willing to share a room with me, provided we could choose our own partners. I was beginning to like the looks of Rob both from a mental and physical perspective.

CHAPTER 10

The following day we were all collected and driven to the house. On the journey after they had picked me up, we collected Rob and another guy by the name of James.

"Hi Nathan, how're things?" asked the jovial Rob, on opening the car door and climbing into the vehicle.

"Fine thanks and you? Are you excited?"

I could sense that he was excited without expecting an answer from him.

James introduced himself to us and then proceeded to explain that he was a banker. It was not that I had pre-conceived ideas as to what bankers should look like, but James seemed to fill my expectations of them. He was tall and thin slightly balding, but not unattractively so. He looked about thirty years old and wore heavy-rimmed glasses, which made him appear slightly nerdish.

When we arrived at the house, we disembarked and James led the way into the house. Rob followed him and then I followed. As I walked behind Rob, I found myself watching the firm ass in front of me as it lifted gently with each step. Rob had a fine ass, but I was sure that he also had an even finer dick. We made our way into the main entrance hall.

"Wow this is not what I expected," I said, walking into the lounge area.

"Why what were you expecting?" asked Rob.

"I don't know. I just didn't expect it to be furnished so well."

In the lounge area were seated six other guys, chatting. These were obviously some of our competition.

"Hi guys," I said walking to where they were seated. "I'm Nathan and this is Rob," I said introducing both of us. I did not include James as he was still wandering around the entrance hall area.

The guys chatting were a tall well-built African American by the name of Bill, a guy of Chinese decent by the name of Lu, two frat-looking guys called Larry and Troy, Greg, who we already knew, and a sun-bleached blond whose name was Chad.

Bill rose to shake hands with me and as he grasped my hand, I felt the crush around my fingers.

"Hi there buddy, I'm Bill, and this here is Chad. As you can see from his tan and sun-bleached hair, he's a beach bum."

"I'm not actually a beach bum," replied Chad, also rising and shaking my hand, "I'm a surfer and run my own surfboard making company."

"That sounds great," I said, smiling at him and shaking his hand.

Soon we were all shaking hands and introducing ourselves and just then James entered the lounge, so the introductions went on a little longer than usual.

"If I look around us, there seem to be nine of us. Who is missing? Anyone know?" asked Rob.

We all looked around, counting the number of people in the lounge. Sure enough, there were nine young men and Frank had said that the competition would involve ten.

"Anyone know who the last guy might be?" I asked.

Shoulders were shrugged and heads shaken as a sign of no-one knowing. "So what are the sleeping arrangements?" I asked.

"Chad and I have paired up," quipped Bill, before anyone else could lay claim to either of them.

"And Nathan and I have agreed to share," responded Rob.

"How about us sharing, Troy?" asked Larry. "I mean it makes sense as we're both college students."

Very quickly, Lu spoke up and asked Greg if he was willing to share.

"I don't have a problem," replied Greg, "if you don't mind me occasionally snoring."

There was a chorus of laughter at the thought of poor Lu having to endure Greg's snoring.

"That looks like you, James and the other guy will have to share," said Bill, shrugging his shoulders as if to say 'bad luck'.

"I've just thought of something," I said to the group, "but are there sufficient bedrooms for us to share?"

"Oh yes," answered Chad. "We've already surveyed the house. It is huge. There are five bedrooms, a bathroom with separate shower, a spare room with a 'NO ENTRY' sign on the door – and it is locked. Then there's the kitchen and a dining room…"

"…You must see the outdoors," chirped Bill, butting into Chad's description of the house.

"There's a beautiful swimming pool, a Jacuzzi, a massive garden that you could be lost in and a tennis court," continued Bill.

"Of course you forgot the high wall surrounding the property," stated Chad. "High enough to prevent snooping or prying eyes."

"Why don't we go out and have a look around, Rob," I asked.

So Rob and I were about to make our way out the front to the swimming pool, closely followed by Greg and James, when we heard a loud voice addressing the whole group.

"Good morning gentlemen and welcome to your new home!"

We stopped in our tracks and all turned to see Frank entering the lounge. We turned and re-entered the lounge area.

"I see you've all met each other and I hope, settled in. It is nice to see you guys again from the last time we spoke to each other, and I want to thank you for accepting the invitation to take part in this reality show. Please guys, take a seat as I want to fill you in on more details on how the show is going to be run," said Frank, referring to us who were on our way to the garden.

We found vacant seats and made ourselves comfortable.

"Right," continued Frank, "the first thing I need to tell you is that from tomorrow, the show starts. That means from midnight tonight, the cameras and microphones will be activated and every move that you make in this house will be monitored. There are cameras in every room of the house, except the toilet, for obvious reasons, so just try to act naturally. I know that to begin with you're going to be self-conscious of all the cameras in your face as it were, but I think you'll become used to them so as to be natural. You might have noticed that there is a room with a 'NO ENTRY' sign on the door – that room is the secrets room. When we want to communicate privately with any one of you, we will call you into that room. It is sound proofed so that no one standing outside of the door will be able to hear what is being said inside of the room. Likewise, if any of you wish to communicate with me or one of my staff, you will have to contact us via the phone in the house and then we will speak to you in the room. Are there any questions so far?" asked Frank.

We remained silent.

"Right then, let me continue. The name of the show is 'Who's the Daddy?'"

Immediately there was a great deal of sniggering from the guys in the lounge.

"Yes, guys, we want to see who among is the Daddy of the group. Now we are not going to be the judges, instead, the public will vote each week and the guy with the lowest number of votes will be eliminated and asked to leave the house. When we have a situation where there are two guys in rooms on their own, they will form the new partnership and become roommates. When I 'auditioned' you, I explained that the prize is fifty thousand dollars. This is an amount not to be taken lightly. You may also have realized that now there are only nine of you, when I had said originally that there would be ten contestants. There are going to be ten of you, but the tenth person is being brought in to add an international flavor to the show."

A general hubbub started among the guys in the lounge, wondering who the international person was.

"Gentlemen, let me introduce you to the final competitor. All the way from France it gives me pleasure to introduce to you, Claude De Ville," said Frank almost majestically.

We all turned to the entrance hall area and in walked a very good-looking, well-built man.

"Oh no!" I exclaimed.

"What?" enquired Rob, on seeing my reaction.

"I don't believe this. I know him. I met him when I was in Paris on a work-related project."

Claude walked into the lounge where a number of greetings were exchanged. I was all smiles on seeing him but I did not let on that I knew him until he came over to me to shake my hand.

"So nice to see you again, Nathan. I think this is going to be fun," said Claude, warmly.

I was a little dumbstruck but I also knew that we had stiff competition from this man. As Claude moved around the group, meeting each person, Rob turned to me.

"Pretty good looking. What's he like, Nathan?"

Quietly, so that the others did not hear, I replied.

"Now that's a daddy. That is serious competition. When we're alone I might tell you about him, but in the meantime, watch out as he's hot!"

I saw a change in the face of Rob. I was not sure whether he had become nervous of Claude or if he had thought Claude was going to be competition for my affections.

"Gentlemen, could I have your attention please!" said Frank. "I'm leaving and the next time you'll see me is when we have a winner. Remember to have fun and try to be yourselves. Claude, I'm sorry that you're the last to arrive as I'm sure that the others have already chosen their roommates, but settle in and enjoy yourselves."

With that, Frank departed, leaving us to either unpack or be acquainted with the other guys. James made his way to Claude to introduce himself and tell him that they were roommates. However, before he could get to him, Chad approached him.

"Hey, James, I was thinking that if you wanted to share with Bill, I'd be willing to change places with you."

James first looked blankly at Chad, and then a smile crossed his face.

"Why?"

"Well I just thought you might enjoy Bill's company."

Again James smiled, seeing how fickle Chad had suddenly become on seeing someone he probably thought either better looking or manlier than Bill.

"Thanks for the offer Chad, but I think I'll take my chances with Claude," replied James who then continued to move towards Claude to introduce himself.

Rob and I had accidentally overheard the conversation between James and Chad and we grinned at each other as this revealed certain qualities about Chad that might be advantageous to us at a later stage.

The balance of the day was spent relaxing and trying to adjust to a new lifestyle of doing nothing, other than enjoying ourselves, and then later that night, we all went to our various bedrooms and settled down to start the 'game' the following morning.

CHAPTER 11

I awoke to feel the sun streaming through the bedroom window and as I opened my eyes, I glanced to my left and saw Rob curled up in bed next to me. He was sleeping peacefully and I slipped from the warmth of the bed so as not to wake him and made my way to the bathroom. When I returned to the bedroom, Rob had awoken and was stretched out in the bed; the duvet only just covering his surprisingly developed chest. To my surprise, I never expected him to look, physically, the way he did.

"Morning," I chirped, "I see you moved in last night."

"Nathan, I'm sorry. What can I say? I hope I didn't do anything I might regret."

"Rob as far as I know, nothing happened and I only knew that you had climbed into bed with me when I woke up now,"

"How did you sleep?" asked Rob.

"I just passed out when my head hit the pillow," I answered. "And you?"

I was tempted to say that Rob could have cuddled up closer to me, but I thought it might be inappropriate to say that, so I merely kept quiet.

"Like a baby, until I woke up feeling cold and maybe that's why I climbed into your bed with you. I hope you didn't mind?"

"Not at all," I answered, but deep down I was sorry that I had been more aware of Rob's presence during the night and perhaps something might have happened between us.

"Are you going down for breakfast, Nathan?"

"I think so, and then I'll shower and shave afterwards. What about you?"

"Sure, let's get dressed and go down."

I pulled on a pair of shorts and Rob did likewise. I could already feel the morning warmth so chose not to put on a shirt and the two of us wandered down the grand staircase to the dining room. When we arrived there, Bill and Lu were seated eating breakfast.

"Morning guys," I said surveying the table with orange juice, fruit, cereals and a coffee pot filled with brewing coffee.

"Who prepared all this?" asked Rob, bewildered by the array of food and knowing that there was no chef or maid to prepare for them.

"Lu did," replied Bill. "I think we've got ourselves a good little chef here."

Lu felt proud of himself and smiled broadly; while Rob and I sat down to join them for breakfast.

"Hey did either of you guys shower this morning?" asked Bill.

"No," I replied. "Why?"

Bill laughed.

"I forgot about the cameras and there I was in the shower sponging myself and soaping up my body…"

"… And…?" Enquired Rob.

"Well when I got to the crown jewels … well they got treated fairly well I think."

"Were you stroking yourself?" I asked, grinning at Bill.

Bill grinned broadly and then added, "Fuck I was so enjoying myself when I suddenly looked up and saw the camera.

We all burst out laughing at the thought of Bill jerking off in the shower.

"So the public saw you jerking?" asked Lu.

"I suppose you could say that," replied Bill.

"Maybe you will get many votes because of that," continued Lu. "The ladies will all vote for you…"

"And the men," chirped Rob, butting in.

"Well, I suppose when you've got it you should flaunt it and I've got plenty to flaunt," said Bill rather wryly.

Both Rob and I glanced at each other, probably both wondering just how big Bill actually was.

"What's it like sharing with Chad?" asked Lu, tentatively.

Bill chuckled to himself before answering.

"Well, let's put it this way; I didn't go to bed early last night and when I did Chad wasn't in the room. I woke up about two or two-thirty this morning to find Chad climbing into his bed having only returned to the room then."

We all had grins on our faces as Bill told us about Chad.

"Do you think he was visiting Claude?" I asked. "You know he wanted to swap rooms with James to share with Claude!"

"It doesn't worry me who I share with; I'm here to win," replied Bill.

Just then, Larry and Troy came into the dining room quickly followed by Greg. They all greeted each other and settled down to enjoy their first breakfast together. Immediately the conversation centered on Chad and whether any of them had seen Chad with one of the other guys, particularly with Claude.

"I did see then standing outside chatting," said Troy.

"When was that?" enquired Rob.

"Oh, I'm not sure of the exact time but most of you had already gone to your rooms," continued Troy.

"I bet you he made a move on Claude," said Bill with a broad smile on his face.

As Bill completed speaking, Claude entered the room looking fresh and ready for the day. He was wearing a Speedo and a white vest and one could clearly see the muscular chest and the bulging crotch in the Speedo. Everyone's attention was drawn to this hulk of a man, including Bill, who was not small either.

"Bon Soir, good morning," said Claude, as charming as ever.

They all reciprocated and continued eating their breakfast.

"Did you sleep well?" asked Greg, rather surreptitiously.

They all turned to await the reply.

"Like a little baby," he replied smiling happily.

"And what's it like sharing with James?" resumed Greg.

"He sleeps like the dead," said Claude.

They began to wonder if James, who slept like the dead, would not hear Chad come into the room and climb into bed with Claude.

Rob decided to go directly to the issue at hand.

"Did you see Chad in the night at all?"

"No, why?"

"We hadn't seen him and Bill said that he came back to their room very early this morning and we wondered if anyone had seen him."

"No," replied Claude.

Immediately minds began to wonder if Claude was telling the truth, but they thought better of it and stopped their questioning there and then. The room fell silent and all busied themselves with their breakfast. Just then, the telephone in the house rang and before anyone could get up from the dining room table, they heard Chad's voice answer the telephone. They remained silent trying to hear what Chad was saying, but very soon they were put out of their misery as Chad entered the dining room.

"Morning guys that was Frank on the line."

"What's he want," I asked.

"He gave me our task for today. We are having a sports day and we are in teams. Each room is competing against the others and each event carries points; the team with the highest number of points at the end, will be declared the winners and receive immunity from eviction."

"That sounds like fun," said Larry, showing the first spark of enthusiasm since he arrived. "So what do we have to do?"

"Frank said that we have to congregate at the swimming pool at 10:00am where we would find a list of events and that we would have to follow the instructions and compete in them," said Chad, reading from a piece of paper on which he had scribbled down the message.

Now there was a general noise as the sports day was discussed and the issue of Chad was no longer the topic for conversation.

"I don't know about you, Rob, but I think we could do quite well. I'm not sure of the other's prowess at sport, but you look pretty sporty," I said, quietly so the others did not overhear.

"Chad being a beach bum might be sporty because he said he was a surfer," replied Rob, "and maybe Bill might have some sporting skills, but I can't see the likes of James or Greg mastering very much. Of course Troy and Larry could be the dark horses, and I don't know about Lu."

Breakfast was completed and all either went back to their rooms to get ready for the sports day of went to shower, walk around the garden or just relax.

Rob and I went back to the bedroom where we pulled on our Speedos, grabbed a towel each and went back down to wait in the lounge. Soon, Bill in a pair of pale blue trunks that encased him very dramatically joined us. One could see his muscular legs and the large package tucked into the front of his trunks. He too had pulled on a vest, which enhanced his muscular physique. I stared at this hunk of a man and thought that he would be good competition for Claude when it came to physical beauty. Others were also arriving in various arrays of swimwear and once all were gathered in the lounge, we made our way out to the garden and the swimming pool.

CHAPTER 12

The garden was an Eden of greenery with tall trees, shrubs and flowering beds scattered all around. The swimming pool was very plain being rectangular in shape and measuring twenty-five meters in length, so it was considered large for a residential property. Around the garden were littered pool loungers, umbrellas and tables. There was one long trestle table shaded by a couple of umbrellas, on which stood glasses and various types of cold drinks and snacks. Also on the trestle table was a clipboard on which was a piece of paper with a list of events written down.

"Who's going to take charge of this?" asked Greg, holding up the clipboard.

"I am," said a voice that seemed to come from some overgrown shrubbery.

We all turned and there appeared Uncle Cecil. Immediately I wanted to run up to him and hug him, but I realized that I might blow my position, so I stood my ground. Obviously, Frank had roped Uncle Cecil in to help him with the show.

"Gentlemen, would you please all gather round," said Uncle Cecil, taking the clipboard from Greg.

At no time did Uncle Cecil acknowledge me or I him. It was as though we never knew each other and I was not about to tell Rob either.

"We are going to have a fun morning with each team competing against the others. Will you please get with your partners?"

Uncle Cecil hesitated as we got our groups together, then he continued.

"Gentlemen, before I tell you of the different events, I want to explain the scoring. There are five teams of two members each and only the top three in each event will get points. There are five points for first place, three for second and one for third place. Obviously, the losers get nothing. We are going to have five events starting with the fifty-meter swim. Now I know some of you might think that fifty meters is trivial, but there is a catch. The first swimmer will have to swim backstroke to the other end of the pool. On reaching that end, they get out of the water and mix a cocktail for their partner who will drink it and then dive into the water and swim back to the start. The first team to complete the whole task wins. Is it clear to all of you?"

Uncle Cecil waited for the instructions to sink in and await any questions, and then he resumed his explanations. "There will be a heat with two teams and then one with the other three and times will be kept for each team. As you can see at the other end of the swimming pool are three tables with glasses, bottles of alcohol and a cocktail mixer on each table. The recipe that you are to follow is also on the table."

"What's the cocktail? Shouted Chad.

"That you'll see when you get to the table. Right we have decided which teams go first. Troy and partner will be up against Nathan and partner."

I glanced towards Rob and smiled, thinking that we could have a good chance to win our race.

"Who's making the cocktail?" asked Rob.

"The choice is yours. I don't mind which leg of the race I do. Are you a fast swimmer?"

"Pretty fast, so let me go first and I'll make the cocktail. Is that OK with you?"

"No problem," I replied, pulling off my shirt and getting ready while Rob headed to the other end of the swimming pool to start the race.

I positioned myself next to the table of drinks mix and saw what recipe was awaiting Rob; it was a Harvey Wallbanger. I saw the vodka, orange juice and the Galliano ready waiting to be mixed, but I was unable to tell Rob at the other end of the pool.

"Are you guys read?" asked Uncle Cecil.

Rob and Troy positioned themselves at the edge of the swimming pool.

"GO!" shouted Uncle Cecil.

Together, Troy and Rob hit the water and began swimming while the others cheered them on. For most of the journey, they were neck and neck, and then it appeared as though Rob was slowly pulling ahead. Rob hit the wall first and pulled himself out of the pool. With water dripping everywhere, including into the cocktail glass, he began to make his version of a Harvey Wallbanger. No sooner had he finished it and handed it to me, than I gulped it down. Larry,

Troy's partner was not far behind me as I dived into the water. It was a strange feeling to have a cocktail halfway down my throat and hitting the cool water. I swam as fast as I could and touched the end wall ahead of Larry. Although it was not a race to see who came first, as it was the time that counted, I felt good and I could hear Rob cheering for me as I saw him jumping up and down with excitement.

Once we had emerged from the pool, the next group of three prepared themselves for their race. When they had finished, with Bill and Chad winning their race, Uncle Cecil delivered the verdict.

"First with five points is Bill and Chad; second and three points is Nathan and Rob; and third with one point are Claude and James."

I was surprised how well Claude and James had done, as I did not thank that James would make an impact at any sporting event.

"Right, gentlemen," said Uncle Cecil, "we now come to our version of the shot put. Each of you will have to throw an article and your combined distances will be added. The team who has the furthest distance will be the winners. Let's move over onto the grass area."

We all followed Uncle Cecil and then we saw the article to be thrown – it was a woman's handbag.

"This is no ordinary handbag, gentlemen; it's weighted down so as to give you some idea of how heavy some women's handbags are."

We lined up one behind the other and threw the bag, which was surprisingly heavy. Uncle Cecil had put a five-kilogram bag of sugar into the handbag.

At the conclusion of the event, the results were announced.

"Five points go to Troy and Larry; three points to Nathan and Rob and one point to Claude and James."

After the second event, it meant that Rob and I had six points, Troy, Larry, Bill and Chad had five points, and Claude and Larry had two points. Poor Greg and Lu were struggling.

"I think we need a handicap in our favor," shouted Greg.

"We now come to the event in which only one person per team can compete, so choose your competitor."

"What is the task?" asked Rob.

Uncle Cecil laughed. "Choose the person first and then I'll reveal the task."

Each team went into a huddle as they tried to puzzle out what the task might be.

I noticed that Uncle Cecil was grinning at me as we huddled and discussed. I wondered what was going through his mind, but something kept making me suggest to Rob that I would do the task.

"But what if it's something you can't do, Nathan?"

"Rob, trust me on this one."

"OK, but if you lose I won't be angry."

"Right, can I please have the five individual contestants," said Uncle Cecil, smiling broadly.

The five of us stepped forward. There was Larry, Troy, Lu, Chad and me. We all stood in a row next to each other, then Uncle Cecil produced a tape measure, which got everyone laughing and wondering.

"Right gentlemen. One criterion which we feel a good daddy should have is a big dick, so drop those swimming suits."

There were embarrassed giggles and pleas of not having to do this, particularly as the cameras would pick it up.

"Gentlemen," said Uncle Cecil, loudly. "Those dropping their costumes face the swimming pool as the main camera is behind you, so the public will only see your asses. Of course when they come to the judging they will be able to assess your assets from having seen you from the back. "

We all bent over and removed our swimming costumes then stood facing the swimming pool while Uncle Cecil walked along the row, measuring each guy's dick. Throughout this, the rest of the group were passing lewd comments and jeering at us.

When Uncle Cecil had completed his job, which he obviously thoroughly enjoyed, we were able to pull our costumes back on.

"The scoring for that section I think we keep as a secret," said Uncle Cecil, jovially.

"No! It's not fair! Tell us!" and many more comments erupted from the others.

Uncle Cecil succumbed to the onslaught of requests and soon divulged the result.

In third place with one point is … Chad; in second place is … Troy and the winner of this section is … Nathan with five points."

Uncle Cecil was beaming broadly with excitement and as we prepared for the next task, he sidled up to me and whispered, "I knew you'd win that, my boy."

Now after three events, Rob and I had pulled into a good lead. We had eleven points while Larry and Troy had eight and Chad and Bill were in third place with six points.

"If I had known what the task was I would have done it said Bill and I reckon we could have won."

"But I can tell you, that Nathan's pretty hung," replied Chad, who had seen Nathan's equipment.

"Maybe I could have beaten you," retorted Claude after hearing Bill's comment.

"Maybe, but I doubt it," was Bill's rebuttal.

"Gentlemen, we have two more events to do, so I think it's time that Lu and Greg got onto the board and scored some points.

"We agree," chorused Lu and Greg together.

"To help our waning friends here, we're making this task easier for them. They are going to get a start ahead of the others."

'Not fair! Why them? We all need a start ahead of the good teams,' were some of the comments being bandied around.

"We are going to have a race around the garden," said Uncle Cecil, "the only difference is that you are to carry your partner. Now before you get excited about it, a few hurdles have to be overcome in order to complete the race. You are going to be using the whole property. The route has been marked out for you and you are not allowed to swap positions during the race, even if you get tired of carrying your partner. So think carefully before you decide. All I will tell you is that there are three obstacles to be overcome in order to complete the race."

Again, the groups huddled for discussion and then they started to climb on each other's backs.

"Gentlemen, I didn't say anything about carrying your partner on your back," said Uncle Cecil sternly.

Everyone looked puzzled.

"You are to carry them in the front of you. In other words, your partner will put his arms around your neck facing you and wrap his legs around your waist."

"But we won't be able to see where we're going?" complained Claude.

"That's part of the idea," replied Uncle Cecil. "You see, the person who is doing the carrying is going to travel backwards and the passenger is going to guide them."

There was uproar from the teams. They were all complaining bitterly that they might fall, and that they could not be expected to overcome obstacles if they couldn't see, and so on. However, no amount of complaining was going to change Uncle Cecil's plan.

"Now as I promised, Lu and Greg will get a thirty second start ahead of the rest."

"Is that all?" queried Greg. "Can't we have at least five minutes?"

"No!" said the fatherly Uncle Cecil. "It's thirty seconds. Right, now get into your positions."

We all climbed onto our partners and readied ourselves for chaos.

I had chosen to carry Rob as I thought he might be lighter than I might. For obvious reasons, Claude and Bill carried their partners and Greg carried Lu. Troy and Larry seemed to be constantly debating who was going to do the carrying.

"Greg and Lu, get ready …GO!" shouted Uncle Cecil.

Off strutted Greg with Lu trying to guide and direct him. Thirty seconds later, with Larry and Troy still arguing, Uncle Cecil set the rest of us off. It really was chaotic as our partners tried to guide us while went moved backwards. It was not long before Rob and I took a tumble and had to rearrange ourselves and orientate our direction again. Bill and Chad seemed to be heading away from the rest of us and seemed very coordinated. It was not long before Bill and Chad had caught up to Greg and Lu who looked as if they were out for a Sunday stroll.

The first obstacle appeared in the form of a large tree log that had to be climbed over. Bill stretched his legs apart and easily maneuvered his way over the log to head off towards the second obstacle,

Claude and James had managed to catch up to Bill and as Claude neared the log, so he saw Bill disappearing around part of the house. The race was on.

Rob and I managed to catch up to Greg and Lu, but very soon Troy and Larry caught up to us and for some time we raced together, but when we reached the log, we managed to overtake them.

The second obstacle was when the teams reached an old oak tree growing in the garden. Hanging from one of the branches of the tree were ropes and attached to each rope was a small bucket filled with water. The object of the hurdle was to untie the bucket and the 'passenger' would have to carry the bucket back to the finish without spilling the water, or at least trying to retain as much as possible.

Bill and Chad reached the tree first and Chad tried to untie the bucket but found it difficult to do that and letting go of his hold around Bill's neck. The buckets were hanging at the level of the carrier's height, so the more Chad battled to untie the bucket; the more Bill got splashed with water in the face.

Claude and James quickly caught up and now Bill was becoming frustrated at Chad's inability to untie the know holding the bucket. Almost at the same time that Claude arrived at the oak tree, so Troy and James arrived quickly followed by Rob and me. Now there was panic as we all fought to untie the knots.

"Come on Chad!" shouted Bill as he staggered under the weight of Chad trying to undo the knot.

As they fought to get past this obstacle, Greg and Lu arrived at the tree. Both men cheered when they realized that they were still in the race.

Now it was Rob's turn to struggle to untie the knot and I was becoming frustrated with him. Water was spilling everywhere and all of us carriers were getting drenched from the buckets of water. Finally, Chad managed to get his bucket loose and he and Bill were again on their way to the last obstacle.

James also managed to get his untied and soon he and Claude were in hot pursuit.

"Come on Rob," I shouted.

"I'm trying," was Rob's exhausting sob.

Larry and Troy gave a cheer when they realized that they had released their bucket and set off after the other two teams.

"Come on Rob, we can't let Greg beat us," I yelled.

Poor Rob was all fingers and thumbs, desperately trying to please me.

Suddenly I felt an extra weight and the bucket came free.

"At last!" I sighed and we were back on the path to the next obstacle.

"I'm so sorry, Nathan," said a subdued Rob.

"Not a problem, at least you got it undone."

I did not want to upset my partner because it was after all a team effort and I was not sure that I would have been able to untie the bucket.

Bill and Chad had now built up a good lead and had reached the third and final obstacle.

On a table lay five hamburgers and the object of the task was that the person being carried had to feed the carrier a hamburger while still hanging onto the carrier, with their bucket. It was therefore, Chad's job to feed Bill.

Bill bent his knees so that Chad could reach a hamburger on the table, then once he had one in his hand; he began to feed Bill, who was trying desperately to gulp down the food without choking.

Claude came stumbling up to the hamburger table and James reached for his hamburger, and then started to feed Claude. It was almost gulp for gulp between Bill and Claude, but eventually Bill managed to swallow the last morsel and then headed off to the finish line.

"Come on Bill," encouraged Chad as they neared the finish, "we're almost there."

As they crossed the finish, Chad leapt from Bill and then hugged him warmly.

Uncle Cecil checked to see how much water they had retained in their bucket and then told them that they were the winners of that event.

Second came Claude and James who were not very far behind Bill and Chad. Then there was a bit of a break before the third team arrived back at the finish and that was Larry and Troy. When Bill saw who had come third, he jumped for joy.

"Chad do you know what this means? It means we're tied in first place with Nathan and Rob."

Once all the remaining teams had returned, Uncle Cecil announced the current positions.

"Tied in first place on eleven points are Nathan and Rob together with Bill and Chad. They are followed on nine points by Larry and Troy and then come Claude and John and Greg and Lu."

I was so disappointed that we had not gained any points, but I was not about to take it out on Rob.

"I'm sorry, Nathan. I know it was my entire fault with those knots."

"No Rob, remember this is a team effort, so you're not the guilty party. Instead of worrying about what has just happened, we need to focus on the last task and make sure we beat Bill. Remember there's immunity for the winners."

Rob smiled at my mention of the immunity, but I knew that deep down he was still angry with himself.

"Gentlemen, you have done wonderfully this morning, but there's just one more task for you to do to see who claims immunity," said Uncle Cecil. "This last task is going to test your general knowledge. Throughout the morning I have been testing your physical prowess, so now it's brain testing time. Each of you will have a slip of paper and as a team; you may confer and then write down your answer on the paper. At the end of the questioning, I'll collect the answers and mark then and then we'll l announce the winners."

Uncle Cecil handed out pieces of paper and pens to the teams and then we settled down to answer his questions.

"Are you ready?" enquired our question master.

'Yes' we all chorused together.

"Right, question number one. Who was the author of 'To Kill a Mockingbird'?"

There was a stunned silence, and then Larry and Troy quietly chattered to each other and then wrote down an answer.

"Question two. According to the ancient wonders of the world, where were the Hanging Gardens situated?"

Again, Larry and Troy were huddled in conversation, but this time so was Rob and I. Bill and Chad had been very quiet throughout the questioning so far, so we wondered if they knew any of the answers.

"Question three. When were the Olympic games held in Atlanta, USA?"

Everyone seemed to be able to answer this, or at least write down an answer.

"That one seemed easy enough," remarked Uncle Cecil. Now for question four. Who composed the music for the ballet 'The Nutcracker'?"

Rob immediately whipped the pen from my hand and wrote down Tchaikovsky.

"Are you sure?" I whispered.

He smiled confidently and nodded his head.

"Question five. The Oscars are awarded for film, but what is the name of the award for Broadway shows?"

I quickly wrote down our answer while most of the other teams seemed to stare blankly in front of them.

"Questions six and seven are two part answers," said Uncle Cecil. "I want to know the names of the two people who first reached the peak of Mount Everest, the highest mountain in the world."

There were blank looks everywhere.

"I'll give you a clue," said Uncle Cecil, seeing all the blank faces. "One was from New Zealand and the other was a Sherpa."

Once he said that I could remember one of them.

"Sir Edmund Hillary," I whispered to Rob.

"Are you sure?"

"Yes, but I can't remember the name of the other guy."

"OK, then write it down."

"Can't you give us another clue?" pleaded Greg.

"No!" I shouted. "We've got one of them."

"Right. Question number eight. What is the name of the very tall tower in Paris?"

"Aargh! Thank you," bellowed Claude.

"Hey that's not fair, Claude's from France so he knows that answer."

"So should you, Chad. It's very famous," commented Uncle Cecil.

We had written down our answer as I remembered the tower from my visit to Paris.

"Question nine. Spell the word 'phlegm'."

"Oh that's easy," shouted Troy, "FLEM."

"Sh!" hissed the other teams.

I looked around the groups and saw how they were discussing the spelling of the word, then I looked at Rob and said, "It's either PHLEM or PHLEGM and I can't think why it's the second one."

"Are you sure it's the second version?"

"Rob, I'm not sure but somehow I think it is."

"Then go for it and write it down.

"Finally, gentlemen, question number ten. What is the name of the producer of the show 'Who's the Daddy'?"

Both Rob and I immediately wanted to say it out aloud but I quickly wrote down Frank's name. I put down our pen and looked around. I was surprised to see teams discussing the final question. Surely, they had heard Frank introduce himself at the meeting.

"Gentlemen, I would like you to write your team's name at the top of your answer sheet and hand them in. You can all go back into the house while I mark these and then I'll reveal the final result to you."

We all thanked Uncle Cecil for taking the time to keep us entertained, and made our way back indoors.

As we entered the coolness of the house, people were conducting what can only be described as a postmortem on the general knowledge quiz.

"Hey Nathan, what was your answer to the question of Mount Everest?" Asked Bill.

"Sir Edmund Hillary," came the reply.

"Never heard of him," muttered Greg.

"And the Hanging Gardens?" continued Bill.

"Babylon," I answered.

"Oh shit!" exclaimed Bill. "I forgot that."

I could see a worried look appear on Bill's face. I was wondering if they had messed up in the quiz, but maybe they were just pretending that they'd got their answers wrong.

After much questioning and answering, Uncle Cecil emerged from the garden and entered the coolness of the house.

"Phew! It's so much cooler here," he said. "Gentlemen, I have the final result for you. These are your positions after the quiz. In fifth place is Lu and Greg."

Every one cheered for them as they had really tried their best throughout.

"In fourth place we have Claude and James."

"Sorry mate," said James apologetically.

"No problem, we make up in other ways," replied Claude.

I wondered what he had meant by that and wondered if perhaps there was something 'brewing' between James and Claude.

"In third place we have Larry and Tory. Well done, boys."

We all applauded them.

"Now we are left with two teams – Bill and Chad and Nathan and Rob who were tied on eleven points each. After the quiz, Bill you and Chad had six answers correct and Nathan and Rob you had … eight answers correct. Therefore, our winners today are Nathan and Rob. Congratulations guys, that means you both have immunity from being evicted this week."

Although the others congratulated us, I could sense that Bill was deeply upset by the loss. Rob and I hugged each other tightly and bounced around the room with joy, knowing that at least for this week we were safe. Bill came over and hugged both of us, and then the others followed suit. I noticed how warmly Claude hugged me unlike the others and this intrigued me, as I wondered if he was coming onto me.

"Gentlemen," said Uncle Cecil, "I must now leave you and I hope that you enjoy the rest of the day and don't forget that on Friday you will be judged by the public and on Saturday evening one of you will be eliminated. Good luck to all of you and I hope to see you again."

With that, Uncle Cecil left the house and the atmosphere began to settle down with some guys heading to their rooms while others lazed about in the lounge.

CHAPTER 13

The evening after the sports day, we all gathered in the dining room for a Chinese dinner made by Lu. It was tasty, nourishing and most enjoyable to all, then after dinner some of the guys remained in the lounge to watch television while Rob and I went up to our room. We knew that the camera in our room was on and actively filming us as we lay on our beds discussing the day and the competition.

"I think we did pretty well today, Rob."

"Thanks to you," said Rob, stretching out on his bed. "But who do you think is going to get the chop and be evicted?"

"Truthfully, I really don't know, but if the public vote on today's performance it will either be Greg or Lu."

"My bets are on Lu going," replied Rob. "If you think about it, he's been in the background since his arrival here."

"True! You've got a point there, but we have to remember that it's not just today that they'll vote on, it also what goes on in the house."

"In that case, I wonder if they were offended by Bill's nude showering scene?" enquired Rob.

"Funny, I don't think they'll get rid of him for that. There are too many people who would have probably enjoyed that and if he's as well hung as I think he might be, they'll keep him in for the titillation factor."

Rob lay there thinking about what I had just said, and then he spoke again.

"If that's the criteria that keeps people in this house then I think you, Bill and Claude will be safe. I reckon you're the biggest guys here, if you know what I mean!"

I laughed loudly.

"You're joking aren't you?"

"No, Nathan, I mean it. Of course you might have to include Troy as he came second in the big dick section."

"Sure. But there was only one from each team. You could also be in the running."

Rob laughed heartily when I said that.

"Oh yes, sure! Me in the same class as you guys, I think not."

"Drop you shorts and let's see."

Rob hesitated; laughing all the while, then he leapt from the bed and dropped his shorts.

"And the jockstrap that you're wearing," I said.

He did exactly what I told him and there Rob stood, buck-naked with his dick flopping between his legs. I looked long and hard at his dick. It was awesome both in shape and in length.

"I reckon you'd give Bill a run for his money. You're no little guy, Rob."

He stood there admiring his dick and fondling his balls then he suddenly realized that the world could be watching him. He leaped back onto the bed and pulled the duvet up over him until just his eyes peeped out from under it.

We both burst out laughing and wondering how many people had seen his little, sorry, his big gaffe.

The idea of having the world watching us was daunting and one had to remember that all the time. We laughed and laughed until I said, "I have to tell the others."

"Don't you dare," pleaded Rob. "It's not funny."

"Hey, listen Rob, before this week's over I reckon every one of us will have revealed ourselves to the public, so stop worrying about it. We are here to be ourselves, and remember the title of the show is "Who's the Daddy.""

"So? Your point is?"

"My point is that the public probably expect a Daddy to be well hung and someone who takes charge of a situation. If that is the criteria, then we'll soon be able to establish who is likely to get voted out and who'll be left."

By the end of the week, I was to be proved right.

At the end of the first week, we received a telephone call from, Frank saying that he wanted to speak to Claude, Bill and Rob in the Secret Room.

"What do you think this is all about?" enquired Claude, as we all sat in the lounge on the Friday evening.

There were a few mutters among the group but no one knew for sure why they had been called.

"Do you think it was because I flaunted my equipment in the shower?" asked Bill.

"Yes!" replied Rob, with a sudden realization. "I also got caught naked in the room on the day of the sports event."

"What were you doing?" quipped Greg, with a glint in his eye.

"Nothing serious," said Rob, suddenly regretting the fact that he had mentioned his nudity.

"Were you measuring your dick?" asked Chad.

Everyone laughed at the suggestion.

I was about to tell them that they were correct, but then I felt for Rob, so I kept my mouth shut.

"Of course not," said an embarrassed Rob.

"Well, you'd better go to the room," I said, trying to get them back to reality.

Bill, Claude and Rob made their way to the Secret Room, closing the soundproofed door behind them. In the room were two easy chairs and a large television set. Bill sat in the one chair, while Claude and Rob tried to share the other. The television set lit up and soon Frank's face appeared on the screen.

"Evening gentlemen."

Instinctively they all replied.

"Gentlemen, this is the first elimination but before I get to that, how has your week been. Bill, you tell me first."

"I think it's been fun. We all had great fun at the sports day and I think that everyone's got on with each other."

"No arguing or fighting?" asked Frank.

"No, not that I know of," replied Bill.

"Now tell me Bill, what happened in the shower?"

There was an embarrassed giggle from Bill before he answered.

"I suppose you're referring to my naked body in the shower?"

"Yes," replied Frank. "You're quite a big guy aren't you?"

"I suppose so, or so I'm told," answered Bill.

"And you Rob, you also seem to like flaunting your size to the public."

Rob blushed profusely.

"I forgot the cameras were on."

"Hmm! Also a big guy," said Frank from the television set. "And you Claude!"

"No! I haven't revealed myself to anyone."

"You didn't have to Claude. The public are not stupid you know. They could establish from your Speedo that you too fit the big boys' club," said Frank with a smirk on his face.

"Well, let me put you three out of your misery; the public love you, whether because of your nakedness or your sizes I don't know, but you three are safe from eviction."

The three broke into smiles and laughs of joy and relief, then Frank spoke again.

"Will you please send the following to the Secret Room: Nathan, Chad, James and Troy?"

Bill, Claude and Rob all left the room happily and made their way back to the lounge where the next group was called. Nathan led the group into the room to find Frank's face still on the television screen.

"Good evening gentlemen, please take a seat wherever you can. How do you think you've done this week?"

Chad was the first to speak up.

"I think I've done quite well."

"Chad, tell me why you wanted to change rooms on the first day. You had been happy to room with Bill and then Claude showed up and you wanted to change. Why was that?"

Chad went silent for a moment.

"I don't really know," he stammered.

"Do you think it was because you preferred Claude?" continued Frank.

"I really don't know," was Chad's only reply.

"Nathan, congratulations on winning the sports day with Rob. That means that you are immune from eviction this week. You may leave the room."

"Thank you Frank," said Nathan, who promptly departed from the room.

"Now James tell me how you think you've fared this week with the public?"

"I don't really know, but I think I've tried to keep my nose out of problems."

"When you say that, have there been problems in the house?"

"No, Frank, what I meant was that I hadn't been running around in the nude."

"Ah! Maybe that is a pity as I think the public would have enjoyed that. Gentlemen, let me put you out of your misery, you're all safe, you may go, but before you do, will you please send me the remaining guys."

Larry, Greg and Lu made their way to the Secret Room, knowing now that one of them was about to be evicted. They entered the room and sat down silently in the two chairs, Lu and Greg sharing a chair.

"Hi guys, how are you all?"

A muttered response was given without anyone of them sounding enthusiastic about being in the room.

"I'm sure that you're well aware that one of you will be going home tonight."

They silently nodded their heads.

"Larry, how do you think you're doing?"

"I think I should be fine. I worked well with Troy and we did well in the sports event, so I'm happy," said Larry.

"What about you Lu?"

"I'm not sure Frank. Greg and I tried our best at the sports but we're not that way inclined."

"Do you think the public would agree with you?"

"Probably."

"And you Greg; do you see yourself as a Daddy?"

Greg laughed timidly and shrugged his shoulders.

"What's that supposed to mean?" asked Frank, the face on the television screen remaining impassive.

"Larry, you're safe so you may leave the room," said Frank.

Larry did as he was told and left.

"That means one of you two guys is going home tonight."

There was a long, drawn out moment of silence, and then Frank spoke once more.

"Lu, the public have decided that you should go. Please pack your things and leave the house."

At that, the television screen went blank and silence fell on the room. Greg looked at Lu and then got up and hugged him, giving him a kiss on the cheek. The two men slowly left the room and headed back to the lounge to inform the waiting group.

"It's me," said Lu, with a half-hearted smile. "I'll be sorry to say goodbye to you guys, but in the short time that I've been here, it's been fun."

They all congregated around Lu to say their goodbyes and then the young Chinese man left.

CHAPTER 14

Although the first week went by almost uneventfully, the second week proved to be more traumatic with regard to relationships. On the Tuesday evening Chad had been in charge of making the dinner, which was quite good and tasty, but he had not washed the dishes after the meal, which was the rule of the house that whoever made dinner had to clean up. Unfortunately, both Bill and Larry felt it was unacceptable that they should clean up after Chad, as it was to be their turn to make the breakfast the following morning.

As Chad sat in the lounge, his feet up on the coffee table, relaxing, Bill and Larry attacked verbally. The arguing and shouting alerted Greg and I to come running to see what was happening. Voices were raised and the more that Bill reprimanded Chad, the more arrogant Chad became. At one stage, Bill grabbed Chad and raised him to his feet so that they were face-to-face, shouting at each other. I was not sure whether Bill was intending to hit Chad, but I thought better than interfering in case I came off second best. Eventually Claude entered the fray and separated the two men, reprimanding both of them for their behavior. To alleviate the tension, I suggested to Greg that we go and wash the dirty dinner dishes while the others calmed down a little.

We had busied ourselves in the kitchen and were just reaching the end of the washing up when Claude, accompanied by Troy, who had also heard the commotion, entered.

"Do you guys need a hand?" enquired Claude.

"No, it's fine, thanks," I answered. "We're nearly finished."

"What's Chad's attitude?" asked Troy, not having known the full outburst.

"Oh it was about the dirty dishes," sighed Greg, drying the last of the dinner plates.

"I notice he's become very lazy in these last few days," continued Troy.

This we all agreed with.

"I have a word with him tonight when he comes back to our room," said Claude, sounding very fatherly.

"If he goes back to your room," I added. "I get the feeling that Chad is on a mission to try to bed each one of us."

There was a peel of laughter from the guys in the kitchen.

"You're joking," replied Greg.

"Well look at the day we arrived and how he and Bill were sharing but then on seeing Claude he suddenly wanted to make changes," I said.

The laughing subsided and they began to nod their heads in agreement.

"Look, it's none of my business who sleeps with whom, but I just thought him very fickle in his manner the way he changed his mind the minute he saw Claude," I stated.

"Let's forget about Chad," said Larry, speaking up for the first time, "at least the kitchen is now clean for us to use in the morning."

That evening when Bill went up to his room, Chad was already in his bed, pretending to be asleep.

"Are you awake Chad?" asked Bill in a not so soft voice that would make sure that should Chad be asleep, he would wake up.

"Hm?" replied a 'dozy' Chad.

"I asked if you were awake!"

"Well, I am now thanks to you."

Bill sat on the edge of Chad's bed and started to speak to him in a fatherly way.

"Listen Chad, if you want to survive in this competition, you need to play ball and keep your nose clean. Remember that the public decide who goes and who stays and if you continue to behave like a spoilt brat, you're not going to be here for much longer and I'm sure that's not what you want."

Chad merely gave a grunt and turned in his bed to face Bill. Bill had already removed his shirt and shorts and was sitting in his briefs on the bed. Chad noticed this and saw the large bulge in the front of Bill's briefs. This attracted his attention and soon Chad's hand rested on Bill's thigh.

"Chad, we all like you. You are a great guy but you come across as being arrogant to some of the guys and this might translate into you being disliked not only by them but also the public. Do you understand?"

Chad's hand slid higher up Bill's thigh and his face took on the appearance of a child being scolded.

"I actually like you and so do others, but you have to get real," continued Bill. "You can't go around ruffling feathers and upsetting people because it's only going to make your name dirt in the end."

Chad's hand reached the bulge and rested on Bill's hefty balls, encased in the white cotton underwear. Chad's finger began to caress the hefty balls and almost instantaneously, Bill began to get an erection, which Chad noticed.

"If you think about it, it actually doesn't take very long to wash up the dirty dishes after a meal, and it's not as if you have to do it every day or night, so play ball with us, Chad and we'll all get along famously."

It appeared as if a tear or two might be welling up in Chad's eyes, but his hand was busily massaging the swollen dick that was straining to escape the cotton briefs.

"Won't you get in next to me," whimpered Chad.

Bill looked down at his young roommate who was lying topless and Bill wondered if Chad was also bottomless. Chad held open the duvet, inviting Bill to join him and in so doing, Bill could see that Chad was naked and had a very substantial hard on. Bill slid in under the duvet and cuddled up close to Chad, their bodies touching and sending electric shock waves through their bodies at the exciting touch. Instantaneously, their lips met and the conversation came to an abrupt end. Their bodies began to writhe in the bed and they fought to take control. Bill's briefs came fluttering from under the duvet and Chad's head disappeared under the duvet, heading towards Bill's large erect cock. As Chad's mouth clamped onto the large, thick cock, Bill sighed loudly and lay back to enjoy the treatment he was receiving.

Soon Chad emerged from under the duvet, sat on top of Bill's cock, and began to bounce up and down as the thick rod slid in and out of his ass.

For about fifteen minutes these two men grunted, groaned switched positions and kissed passionately until Bill shouted that he was about to shoot his load. Both erupted together and almost immediately after both men reaching their climax, silence took over the room and they both fell asleep in each other's arms. As the bedroom light had remained on throughout their passion, the public probably would have applauded the two men's prowess and stamina.

The following morning when Bill went down to make breakfast; he had a satisfied smirk across his face and a spring in his step.

Later that day, Frank called Bill and Chad to the Secret Room.

"Oh shit!" exclaimed Chad. "I think we're in trouble."

"Hi guys how are both of you?" enquired the voice of Frank as Bill and Chad sat meekly in the Secret Room.

"Fine thanks," echoed the two men.

"I need to speak to you about last night," resumed Frank. "It appeared as if there was some problem about the dirty dishes?"

Both men simply nodded.

"You know the rules of the house; that whoever makes the dinner has to wash the dishes afterwards."

Again, they both nodded.

"Chad you chose not to do so and therefore you created a problem in the house."

Chad hung his head in shame.

"Because of that we feel that to set an example we need to punish you," said Frank, his voice sounding sterner.

Chad looked up towards the camera in the room.

"We've decided that you are going to be eliminated at the end of the week."

Chad looked stunned. He felt this harsh punishment.

"People have to learn that there are rules and they need to abide by them," said Frank, not mentioning anything about Chad and Bill having sex together. "Thank you guys, that's all. You may leave the room now."

Chad and Bill emerged from the Secret Room, both looking a little forlorn and dumbstruck.

"Wow, that was harsh," said Bill as they neared the lounge area.

Chad was stunned into silence.

"Hi guys," said a chirpy Larry, who was arriving back from a swim. "The water's so refreshing. Why don't you join us for a swim?"

He noticed that Chad seemed a little subdued and asked what the problem was but Chad merely evaded the question and headed back to his room.

"We've just been called into the Secret Room," replied Bill, "and Chad was reprimanded for his behavior last night."

Bill was not sure whether he should mention the form of punishment to Larry, but then chose to keep quiet about it.

By the end of the week, the group found it strange that they had not been given a task to do and wondered how the voting was going to take place.

On the Friday morning, as they all sat eating a hearty breakfast, the telephone in the house rang and Rob went to answer it. A little later, he returned to the dining room to tell the others the news.

"Guys, listen up! That was Frank and I have some news for you; some good and some bad. The good news is that Frank is going to announce a Daddy of the Week and now for the bad news. This is how the voting is going to take place this week. Apparently we are going to have to vote among ourselves for two people we think should be evicted…"

There was an immediate uproar of complaints from the men. There was mutterings and moaning from all of them.

"Hang on guys!" shouted Rob to quieten them down. "There's something else as well. They have decided that three people are going to be voted off.

"Three! But you said we had to vote for two!" exclaimed everyone is disbelief.

"Chad cannot be voted for as he's already one who they have decided will go."

"What do you mean?" I asked.

Rob looked towards Chad.

"Apparently you know about that."

Chad nodded, and then Bill spoke up.

"Chad and I were summoned to the Secret Room the other day and Frank informed Chad that he would be evicted."

Again, there were mutterings from the others.

"OK guys, let me finish," said Rob, continuing with his conversation. "After breakfast we each have to go, one by one into the Secret Room and tell Frank who we think should be voted off. The idea is that it remains secret as to who you vote for. Once the votes have been counted, the two we have voted to go, will be evicted along with Chad. Nathan, you have to go first and then Frank will tell you who to call afterwards."

They had a little time to think before the breakfast dishes were removed from the dining room and the voting began.

I went into the Secret Room and faced the camera.

"Morning Nathan," said Frank's voice, "how are you today?"

"Fine thanks Frank."

"And how are you doing?"

I laughed a little.

"Fine, thanks."

"Are you getting on with everyone? Any one person that you're getting along with more than the others?"

"I suppose Rob and I are very close," I replied.

"That's great. Rob seems a very nice young man; someone that I think would be good for you," continued Frank, "but remember why you're here, Nathan, it's to see who the Daddy is."

"Yes Frank I understand."

"I'm glad that you understand, and do you think you have what it takes to be the Daddy of the house?"

"Absolutely."

"And what about Rob? Do you think he could be a good Daddy?"

"Sure. He's make a very good Daddy as well."

"Well, Nathan, we can't have two Daddies in the house you know!"

I was not sure what Frank was getting at but I did pick up that he wanted to see me more in control and taking charge.

"So who are you voting off, Nathan?"

I hesitated for a moment, thinking carefully, and then I answered.

"Larry and Troy, Frank."

"Right so that's a vote against Larry's and Troy's names. Thanks Nathan. Please send in the next person."

I left the Secret Room feeling a little regretful that I had to vote off a friend but it was after all a game.

"Next!" I exclaimed as I entered the lounge where everyone was gathered.

Troy was the next to enter the Secret Room.

"Who did you vote for?" whispered Rob to me.

I looked around to see if anyone was watching me, then I leant close to his ear and whispered, 'Larry and Troy'. He seemed somewhat surprised by my vote and had that querying look on his face.

"Larry could be a threat," I whispered again.

Then Rob's expression changed slightly as the thought sank in. When it came to Rob's turn, he glanced once at me and then left.

"Morning Rob, how do you think you're doing in the house?" asked Frank.

"Great thanks Frank."

"And how do like Nathan? You seem to be getting on well with him."

"I really like him, Frank. He seems a genuine sort of guy."

"Do you see yourself as the Daddy of the house?"

"Well there's some stiff competition here, but I think I could be."

"You sound a little hesitant, Rob."

"Well, it's just if you consider Claude, Bill and Nathan – they're all hot guys."

"Hm! Right who do you vote for?"

Rob remembered what I had said then he spoke up.

"Larry!"

"And who else, Rob?"

"I think Claude."

"Fine, thanks. Please send in the next person."

Rob returned to the lounge and sat down next to me, grinning.

"And that grin?" I queried.

"I voted the same as you did, except I also put Claude down," replied Rob.

I too grinned, hoping that there would be sufficient votes to get rid of Larry, but did not think that Claude would be voted out.

At the end of the voting, Frank called Rob back into the Secret Room to give him the verdict. He then returned to the lounge to explain to the guys who the Daddy of the Week was and who was to join Chad in being evicted.

"Guys, the Daddy of the Week is Bill."

The group all clapped and congratulated Bill but some wondered how he had been chosen. Of course, Bill puffed out his chest and felt very proud of himself.

"The persons to join Chad in being elimination are ... Larry and Troy."

Larry had a very forlorn appearance and Claude seemed somewhat disappointed that the group had voted his roommate. Somehow, Troy's reaction was not like that of Larry's.

After this announcement, the group broke up and went their various ways; Rob and I went out to the pool area to lie in the sun and swim.

"Personally, I think Chad deserved to go even though I also voted for Larry."

"Why's that?"

"I just think he's bad news and ought to go."

Just then, Claude arrived at the pool and lay on his towel next to Rob and I.

"What do you guys think of the voting choice?"

I was aware that Larry, being Claude's roommate, might be the one that he did not want voted out and I was not about to say that I had voted for Larry or Troy as well, not to Claude.

"It's a difficult one, Claude," I replied hoping not to be drawn into the conversation about Larry.

"I can't think why people would vote for Larry because he's such a decent guy. He's harmless and between us, very sexy too," said Claude lowering his voice for the last comment.

Rob and I glanced at each other, not knowing what to say. I had not looked at Larry in the same light that Claude had.

"I suppose you could say that," answered Rob. "I mean about the sexy part."

"He has such a fine body," resumed Claude, "and I think he could make a very good lover, you know."

Maybe there were things beginning to happen between Claude and Larry, and we were now in the process of breaking that up.

"Hey! Let's not get too involved in thinking about the vote; let's swim," I said, jumping up and diving into the swimming pool.

Both Claude and Rob quickly followed and soon the conversation changed to other things not related to the people in the house. It was during our splashing around in the pool that Claude let slip about him and I in Paris.

"Did I hear correctly that you guys knew each other before coming to the house?" questioned Rob, with a sense of shock in his voice.

"Purely business," I replied. "I had to go to Paris on business and that's where we met."

"Oh!" replied a somewhat dumbstruck Rob.

I wondered what was going through his mind at that moment. Had we revealed something that could have dire consequences for Claude and me? I began to wonder if Rob was thinking that perhaps Claude and I had enjoyed an affair together in Paris; of course, he would have been right, but I was not going to admit it and I hoped that Claude would keep quiet as well. I then noticed that Rob suddenly decided he had enough swimming and returned to his towel while Claude and I remained in the water.

"Claude," I whispered, so that Rob would not hear. "I think we better keep this quiet about us. If anyone asks, we did business together in Paris and that was all. OK?"

Claude smiled broadly.

"Of yes, mon amie, we sure did business together!"

I knew precisely what he meant and we both smiled. After some time, I returned to my towel next to Rob and lay down without speaking. Rob was lying on his stomach with his face turned away from me, so I assumed that he was either angry or upset. It had not been five minutes of lying next to Rob, when he stood up, gathered his towel and headed back into the house. I waited a while then followed and went up to our room. On entering, Rob had stripped off his Speedo and was lying on his stomach on his bed.

"Rob," I asked, "What's the matter?"

There was no reply.

I sat down on his bed next to him and looked at his smooth, taut, naked body.

"Speak to me."

Nothing!

I lowered my hand onto the small of his back and felt his warmth, then unconsciously as I spoke, so my hand drifted onto his bubble butt and I caressed it tenderly.

"Please talk to me. Did I say something to hurt you? All I said was that Claude and I met on business in Paris."

I continued massaging his bubble butt and then my hands moved up to his shoulders, massaging them.

"Please talk to me."

Suddenly Rob turned over onto his back. His face had tears stained on his cheeks and his eyes were red from crying, but then my eyes trailed down his smooth, taut body and saw the he had an erection. He did not seem to worry about the fact that I was struck by his beauty and erection.

"And this?" I asked looking at his swollen, hard cock and smiling at his beautiful face.

"Don't joke," replied Rob in between sobs.

I could not resist what I did next, but my hand trailed over the length of his erect cock and it felt good both for me and for him as we both sighed together.

I was not interested in talking now that I say the state he was in; aroused and wanting some pleasure from me. My mouth sank onto the tip of his cock and then sank lower over his thick shaft until his whole cock was encompassed by my mouth and throat. There was no more talking until I heard Rob's breathing increase and a sigh was emitted from his throat. I knew he was coming and it pleased me. As he slowly returned from his climax, his tears had stopped and were replaced with a slight smile. I let go of his cock and kissed him gently on the lips.

"Rob, you've got nothing to worry about. I'm here to look after you," I said tenderly, putting my arms around him. "May I lie here next to you?"

He shuffled over his bed to allow me room to get on the bed and we lay together in each other's arms, silently.

As we lay there it crossed my mind that perhaps Rob was falling for me and that he might have been a little jealous of Claude, but in my heart I was sure that Rob had nothing to fear. I was being drawn closer and closer to him each day.

CHAPTER 15

At the end of week three, Bill was once again chosen as Daddy of the Week and there seemed to be some concern on the part of Claude and me. I was trying to understand why he was winning the vote each week and when we had our weekly chat to Frank, I brought up the topic.

"Frank can you tell me how come Bill gets voted Daddy of the Week each week? What are the rest of us not doing?"

"Nathan, you must understand one thing, I don't choose the Daddy of the Week. Public voting does that. The only thing I can think of is that he is popular with the men and women out there because of his good looks and, let us be honest, he is pretty well hung. Wouldn't you agree?"

"Sure he's got a big dick but is that the only criteria on which we're chosen?"

"Of course not," replied Frank, "but you have to show more authority, more domination, for example."

"Meaning?"

"Strut your stuff; make yourself wanted by all the men there and not just Rob; be popular; be sexy and above all flaunt your body for the public."

This was not in my nature and I was not sure how this would affect Rob, who was very close to me. I contemplated speaking to Rob and explaining to him why my behavior might change and hope that he would understand, but more importantly, I did not want to hurt his feelings.

"Nathan, only you know whether you want to win this competition or not."

"I'd like to, Frank."

"Well then, you know what you must do, otherwise the public are not going to favor you and you might find yourself being eliminated. It might even be a good idea to reveal your sexual appetite on camera, like you and Rob did a few days back."

"You mean…!"

"Yes Nathan we all saw you and Rob together in your room. The only difference was that yours wasn't as dramatic as when Bill and Chad made out."

I was somewhat taken aback. Sure, I was aware that the house was full of cameras, but I had been lulled into a sense of self-security and forgot about the world seeing us at it. Now that Frank had raised this point, I was unsure as to what I should do. Did I need to 'change' my personality so to speak or remain my humble self? I decided to speak to Rob.

"Rob, I need to speak privately to you. Let's go for a walk in the garden."

As we ventured out into the lush green garden and wandered among the trees, Rob sensed that there was something bothering me.

"Rob, how do you feel about me?"

"What are you getting at, Nathan?"

"I just want to know how you feel about me, that's all."

"I've told you before, I like you very much."

"Okay, let me put it to you this way. Would you be offended if my personality or behavior changed in any way?"

"I really don't understand."

"I had a chat with Frank and he said if I wanted to stand a chance of winning this competition I needed to become more authoritative, more domineering."

"So, what's the point?"

"I was just a little worried that you might find a change in my behavior off-putting."

"Does this competition mean so much to you," asked Rob, after a moment's hesitation.

I paused and thought about his comment. How important was this competition to me? Did I need confirmation from the public that I was a daddy, or did I have the confidence within myself to be a daddy?

"You're absolutely right, Rob. This competition does not mean all that to me. I am comfortable within my own skin about my abilities.

Rob smiled on hearing these words.

"Why are you smiling like that?" I questioned.

"You don't have to prove to me how you can be a daddy and dominate others nor do you have to prove to anyone that you really are a daddy, but at the end of the day, the decisions are yours. One thing I will tell you, is that no matter what you feel, I'll always back you on it."

I was truly touched by Rob's comments, so much so that I hugged him there under the trees and kissed him passionately.

"So what are you going to do?" enquired Rob, still holding onto me.

"I don't know, but I have to think about it, Rob."

We wandered back to the house and went to lie next to the pool. As we lay there, I looked at the other guys who were also at the pool, trying to weigh up each man and assess how much of a daddy each one was. Once I had done that, it became clear to me that only Bill and Claude could be considered daddies in my estimation, but another thought had crossed my mind; what was I to do if I chose to leave the competition. What would Frank think of me for that matter? In fact, what would Uncle Cecil think? Was I a loser in their eyes? I turned once more to Rob.

"Rob," I whispered, "I've been giving it some thought and I think I'm going to leave the competition."

"What are you talking about? You have every chance of winning it, so why give up now?"

"I don't need to prove anything to myself, Rob. It's been fun doing the competition, but what's in a title? What's more important is what's in you as a person and I know what I want in my life."

Rob stared blankly back at me and I wondered what was going through his mind. Eventually he spoke up.

"And what do you want in life, Nathan?"

"That depends on you, Rob. What I really would like is to settle down with someone who understands me and my way of life and accepts me for who I am."

"So why should it depend on me? I have no say in your life and the decisions that you might make."

"Well, maybe not at the moment, but I sure would like you to be there to help me make some of those decisions."

"Are you saying what I think you're saying, Nathan?"

"If you would be interested, I'd like to live my life with you, but you'll have to accept both Frank and Uncle Cecil – after all they are a part of my life too."

Rob beamed broadly and I could see tears welling up in his eyes.

"But I don't expect you to leave the competition just because I am," I continued. "Not a word about this to anyone as I will have to speak to Frank about leaving. I also need to find out what the rules of the competition are."

"I won't say anything, Nathan, but when are you thinking of speaking to Frank?"

"Tonight," I replied.

That evening I went into the secret room and spoke privately with Frank, explaining my feelings not only about myself but also about Rob and the competition. I was surprised to find that he was completely behind me in my decision and was more than willing to accommodate my wishes.

At the end of the week, when the Daddy of the Week was announced, it came as a shock to me, and a few of the guys, to hear that I had been named Daddy of the Week, and I was certain that it had something to do with my decision to leave the show. At the same time it was announced that I would be leaving the competition of my own choice.

Both Bill and Claude were shocked by my announcement, but both respected my decision and understood the way I felt.

Interestingly, Bill handed me a piece of paper with his contact details written on it and said should I ever want to meet up he would be very keen to do so. I also felt that he did have an interest in me, for whatever reason and I had to admit that I still found him intriguing if not appealing.

At the end of the week, I had packed my bag and was ready to leave, but unbeknown to me, Rob had arranged with the other guys in the house to have himself voted out so that he could accompany me, which I thought was very touching on his part.

And so, my escapade in the show came to an end, but not my life. This was now the start of a new era; one in which Rob would form part of my life and also be in the lives of Frank and Uncle Cecil, who soon had Rob 'sucking sherbet'. I have been duly informed, from those around me, that Rob finds me a loving, caring daddy who understands his needs and desires, as much as he understands mine. That when Frank, Uncle Cecil, Rob and I get together, our roles as daddy's and sons change to suit the occasion but when we get to our home and Rob and I get into bed together, my boy knows his place.

ABOUT THE AUTHOR

Lew Bull is a South African living in Johannesburg and has been published in a number of short story anthologies as well as having had nine novels and two collections of his own short stories published by Nazca Plains. He has also written a play called "Stark Raving Naked".

He has recently retired after twenty-nine years of being involved in education, during which time he was awarded a doctorate in education and a Licentiate from Trinity College, London. He and his partner are currently in their sixth year of being together and he still likes to travel and write erotica.

tales

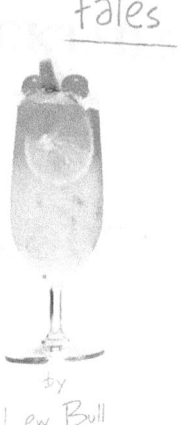

by

Lew Bull

ROUGH CUT

LEW BULL

A NOVEL BY
Lew Bull

Wet, Wild
and Willing

The sexcapades of a single man

MYSTIQUE

LEW
BULL

Power
Buddies

a novel by
LEW BULL

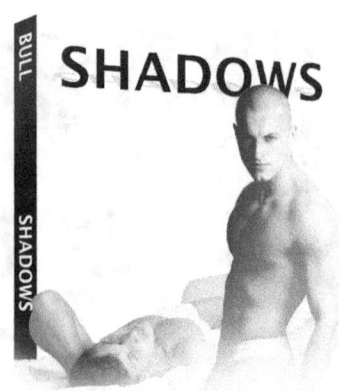

SHADOWS

A NOVEL BY
LEW BULL

A BONER BOOK

THE SLAVE OF
APOLLO

LEW BULL

SWEETMEATS

CHILDREN AREN'T BORN WITH PREJUDICE: THEY GET IT FROM ADULTS

SWEETMEATS

LEW BULL